240

12

Hopes and Fears

Hopes and Fears

PETER TURNBULL

First edition published in Great Britain in 2004 by
Allison & Busby Limited
Bon Marché Centre
241-251 Ferndale Road
London SW9 8BJ

http://www.allisonandbusby.com

A catalogue record for this book is available from
the British Library.

10 9 8 7 6 5 4 3 2 1

ISBN 0 7490 8322 0

Printed and bound in Wales by
Creative Print and Design, Ebbw Vale

Peter Turnbull is the author of nineteen previous novels and numerous works of short fiction. He worked for many years as a social worker in Glasgow before returning to his native Yorkshire.

Chapter One

Thursday, 1st of August, 10.33 hours – 18.00 hours
in which a corpse is warmed.

The man believed himself to be cursed. He was cursed that
it was his destiny to discover bodies, dead bodies. Human
of course...not for him the gentle curse of constantly coming across the remains of small creatures, rather for him the
curse of coming across corpses of the highest primate.
Tragedy had blighted his childhood, not only in that his
highly strung mother had killed herself, but more so in that
he, eight years old, had run home from school delighted
with the good marks he had achieved in a test and had discovered her, sitting in her favourite armchair, with a white
labelled supermarket bag over her head. It seemed to
become the hallmark of his life. His brief spell as a rifleman
in Her Majesty's Service proved itself to be an unremark-
able three years – save for discovering the body of Rifleman
Mills who had hung himself in the latrines. His worthwhile
career in the ambulance service came to an abrupt end when
he and his crewman attended a road traffic accident to discover his son among the fatalities. Mother, army friend,
first born, and now this. The one compensation about this
corpse was that she was unknown to him, but the curse
continued because again, he was clearly the first person to
find her, at the very least, he would be the first to raise the
alarm, but given that he had crashed through dense under-
growth to reach this location, he felt he was the first to find
her. The man turned slowly away, groping for his mobile as
he did so. He personally detested mobile phones, "brain
fryers" as he referred to them, hated their selfish use on rail
journeys, but he conceded their worth in summoning help

in emergencies and, as in this case, raising the alarm when in a remote area. He dialled 999 hoping he wasn't in a 'shadow' and that his phone's signal would be picked up. It was.

"Police," he said when the call was answered.

"What is your name and address?"

The man provided the information. He had been a member of the emergency services. He knew the procedure.

"Police," a second voice said, calm yet authoritative.

"I want to report a dead body."

"Yes, sir. Where?"

"Well, it's in the woodland on the north side of Stillwater Lake...it's a hike from the road. If you send a patrol car along the road that runs alongside the lake, tell them to look for a silver Citroën."

"Silver Citroën?"

"Yes, that's my car, parked in a lay-by."

"Registration number?"

The man gave the number of his car, reeled it of as mechanically as he once used to reel off his service number.

"I'll make my way back there and wait for the officers."

"Very good."

The man switched off his mobile and slipped it back into his pocket and began to crash back through the bracken and saplings, all plans for that day wholly abandoned. He drove a determined path through the wood, holding the knapsack strap with his left hand and his binocular case with the other, until he emerged at the roadside whereupon by sense of direction he turned right, enjoyed an easier stroll under bright sunlight, with golden fields to his left, along the grass verge, to where he had parked his car. He waited by the car, enjoying the day, the weather, the scenery, having reached that stage in life where he had absorbed the fact that time was limited and he now found great joy in simple pleasures. A combination of summer weather freshened by recent rainfall in his beloved Vale of York being one such.

The police car arrived several moments later, driving at speed with headlights on, but without a lapping blue lamp, not being needed in the light traffic of a rural road in mid-week. The police vehicle slowed and halted behind the silver Citroën. Two serious-faced constables got out of the car.

"Mr Handy?" asked the officer who had been driving.

"Yes. I phoned you."

"A body?"

"In the wood." He noticed that both officers wore white shirts, serge trousers, dark shoes. "You might need your tunics," he added. "Not just because it's chilly in the wood, it's wet from this morning's rain. You'll get soaked."

The officers glanced at each other and turned back to the parked car and retrieved their jackets.

"What were you doing in the wood, Mr Handy?" The driver of the police car buttoned up his tunic. He saw a man with a silver beard, a black baseball cap, combat jacket, corduroy trousers and stout boots.

"I'm a 'twitcher'," Handy smiled and tapped his binocular case. "A birdwatcher. Quite harmless...a bit off centre perhaps, but utterly harmless. A pair of red kites has nested in a tree on the opposite bank. The best view to be had is from this side of the lake...utterly uninterrupted line of sight, only a hundred yards away, which in twitching terms is right on top of them, especially with powerful lenses."

"I see."

"Actually, I won't need them today, not now." He unlocked his car and put the binoculars and the knapsack inside and locked it again, leaving one window open by a few inches. "Won't need my lunch either," he added. "Well, it's about three hundred yards along the road before we turn into the wood. But this is the only place you can park your car without leaving it on the road as such."

"Three or four hundred yards," the driver echoed. "We'll take the car. It's a question of time."

Fifteen minutes later the two constables stood looking at the body. Handy, having declined to go the last few feet, had stopped, stood aside and pointed to an oak, and said, "Other side of yon. I don't want to see it again. In fact, if you don't mind, I'll go back home. That's me for the day. You know where I am if you want to talk to me, but I saw nothing nor nobody else." The constables had strode on, and Handy, having interpreted that as consent to withdraw had done just that. There was shopping to be purchased and the vegetable patch to be dug. The red kites could wait.

George Hennessey pushed a low branch aside and was showered with rainwater, clean, fresh summer rainwater. In other circumstances he would be pleased that the woodland and the crops in the Vale received such life-giving goodness in what was held to be a particularly dry summer. He walked steadily through the strong scented woodland towards the blue and white police tape which had been tied around four trees and delineated a box area of about twenty foot square. Solemn faced constables stood outside the tape, as did Somerled Yellich who nodded and doffed his hat as Hennessey closed to within speaking distance.

"Morning, sir."

"Yellich." Hennessey halted at the tape and saw a heavy-duty plastic sheet covering a slightly raised area. He turned to Yellich and raised his right eyebrow.

"Adult deceased of the female sex." Yellich reported, by then well used to his senior's idiosyncratic manner of requesting information or explanation depending on the particular set of circumstances. "Late teens, or early twenties, north European by racial group. Dr Mann pronounced life extinct at..." Yellich hurriedly consulted his notebook, "at 11.30am this day. He's just left, in fact, sir."

"Yes...I thought I recognised him, he was driving towards York as I arrived...thought it was he."

"Dr D'Acre has been asked to attend. There are no visible injuries."

"Found by?"

"A gentleman."

"Walking his dog?"

"Not this time...new one on me this time...a birdwatcher. Constables Graff and Day were the first police at the locus, took the gentleman's details. He was picking his way through the wood to get to the lakeside, he wanted to look at a bird's nest on the other side of the lake, reckoned this would be the best vantage point and stumbled upon...upon her." Yellich nodded at the plastic sheet.

"Young, you say?"

"Very. Adult, but young."

"Show me."

Yellich lowered himself under the blue and white tape and lifted the plastic sheet. He revealed a deathly pale corpse of a woman who Hennessey saw was just as he said, naked, late teens or early twenties...slender of figure, high cheekbones, short blond hair...a young woman, who in life would have had the confidence of knowing that she would be considered beautiful. A very fortunate life had been cruelly snuffed out. He nodded his thanks and Yellich gently lowered the sheet back over the body displaying, in Hennessey's view, proper deference towards the deceased. He knew that soon, in a household close or distant, home or abroad, all hope would be dashed, to be followed by much weeping, much, much weeping. "So young," he said.

"Yes, boss." Yellich pursed his lips. "She had so much to live for...many women would kill to have looks and a figure like that."

"Which is the downside to being attractive, makes you a target as well as an object of affection. She couldn't have walked home alone, at night anyway."

"Did Dr Mann mention anything at all?"

"He did, yes, he said the body was very cold."

"Cold?"

"Yes, boss. He said it would be something Dr D'Acre would pick up immediately...but she is chilled, a lot colder than she would be if she had been killed a few hours ago, even the absence of clothing wouldn't explain the low temperature and the warm weather would have impeded a temperature drop."

"Yet no sign of decay?"

"From a lay perspective, sir, none...no decomposition at all."

Yellich and Hennessey held eye contact then Yellich said what both men were thinking. "She's been kept in a deep freeze. She could have been murdered years ago."

"Yes...it is the only possible explanation. But that helps us."

"It does?"

"Well, yes...ponder if you will, a corpse laid in a deep freeze, then removed. When the corpse was found it was still frozen, what does that tell you?"

"Local, sir," Yellich smiled. "Yes, of course. If it had been transported any distance it would have thawed."

"That's my thinking. I also think... Oh, Dr D'Acre."

Yellich turned to his left, following Hennessey's gaze, and saw a slender woman, confidently striding towards them. She wore a light summer raincoat, carried a black

Gladstone bag...had close cropped hair.

"I also think it means the body was moved in panic."

"Panic?"

"Well, if not out and out panic, then fear or under unexpected time pressure. Look around you, what do you see?"

"Woodland 'lovely dark and deep', as Robert Frost would have said."

"Who?"

"An American poet – I've just discovered him – found a copy of his poems among Sara's books."

"Alright, so as you, or he says, 'lovely dark and deep', but leaving a corpse here tells you what?"

"Didn't want it to be discovered?"

"Yes, my thinking too, or that the person intended to return and dispose of it more efficiently. There is no pathway about here, the vegetation is thick, nobody wanders in here unless upon a set purpose...as in disposing of a body or creeping up on a birds nest. This is progress, Yellich, the person who did this is under pressure. Helps us..."

"Yes, boss. I can see that."

"Helps us enormously." Hennessey turned to Dr D'Acre and he too doffed his hat. "Morning, ma'am."

"Good morning, Chief Inspector, Sergeant Yellich." Dr D'Acre had a soft speaking voice. She wore no make-up, save for a trace of very pale lipstick. "What do we have?"

Hennessey told her. He also mentioned Dr Mann's observation about the temperature of the body to which Dr D'Acre said, "Now that is interesting, more from your point of view than mine, but interesting."

"Yes, ma'am, we were discussing the implications of same as you arrived."

"I bet you were, said implications being huge, large and significant." She lowered herself and slid under the police tape and, in doing so, showed her physique to be lithe and muscular. She peeled the sheet away and groaned. "Oh, I know all human life is sacrosanct, but when the victim is youthful, has so much ahead of her...it just seems to unfair."

Hennessey and Yellich remained silent, watching as Dr D'Acre knelt and laid her hand on the arm of the corpse.

"My!" she withdrew her hand. "It's so cold, it almost stings. This corpse has been chilled." She turned and looked up at Hennessey. "I mean chilled...deep frozen. The mortuary keeps its cadavers at a temperature of –1°C, all that is needed to prevent decomposition, but this...she has been encased in a block of ice. No noticeable injuries. No sign of decomposition. She was frozen upon death, she may even have been frozen to death...but I don't want to speculate at this stage...so time..." She glanced at her watch, "11.55, 1st of August. I'll take a ground temperature." She opened the Gladstone bag and took out a thermometer, which she laid on the ground, ensuring the end was in direct contact with the topsoil. She stood as the mercury settled. "The rectal temperature is hardly worth taking, it will register as freezing, but I'll take it anyway for form's sake. The difference between ground and rectal temperature indicated possible time of death which I know you'll want, Chief Inspector." She looked at Hennessey but her face betrayed no emotion, she was detached, determined, focused.

"Strangely enough, not in this case, ma'am. Before you arrived here we, Yellich and I, agreed that if Dr Mann was correct and the corpse had been frozen then...well...she could have been murdered months, years ago."

"Yes."

"I would be more interested in finding out when she was left here. Any indication?"

"Well, as I have said before, time of death, time when the corpse was deposited at any given locus is most often a matter of common sense than scientific calculation. But this weather...very warm...and what a merciful shower of rain we had this morning...the corpse is still frozen at midday. Two things can be deduced from that: firstly, it was deposited after dark last night, and secondly, before dawn this forenoon. Any earlier and there would be signs of thawing and in the darkness, because logically you would need darkness to move the body from a motor vehicle – it couldn't have been conveyed here by any other means. I would have thought though, here I trespass on your expertise."

"Oh, trespass all you like, ma'am."

"Not just because of the darkness, of course, but because there are few folk around in the dead of night. No sign of thawing means she wasn't dipped into the deep freeze and taken out again. She was kept in there for a long time – she's frozen through. Helps though, captures her at time of death, medically speaking...any alcohol or other toxins will be frozen in her bloodstream, last meal in her stomach...it'll all be there...local..."

"I'm sorry?"

"Well, she wasn't in the motor vehicle long enough for her body to be warmed by the heat within said vehicle. She wasn't in the vehicle for above an hour, so driving so as not to attract attention...What do you think?"

"About thirty miles from here, max."

"The other thing...you know how some corpses are left to be discovered, for the shock value?"

"Yes. Yellich and I believe this corpse was not meant to be found for a long time – if ever – and was probably moved in a hurry."

"Yes," Dr D'Acre nodded, "but the point I make is that the person who deposited our young friend here didn't drive around looking for a likely dumping place, otherwise the corpse would have begun to thaw. He, she, or they knew that this wood existed."

"Local knowledge."

"Would be my opinion." Dr D'Acre knelt and noted the ground temperature reading. "Well, as I would have thought, a cool 3°C. I'll take the rectal reading for forms sake, as I said, then if you have finished, the body can be conveyed back to York District Hospital." She turned the corpse over.

"Have we finished yet, Yellich?"

"Yes, sir. SOCOs have finished, all photographs taken."

"All finished, ma'am."

"Good. I'll do the post-mortem after lunch...warm her over lunch."

"How will you do that ma'am...out of interest?"

"Warm bath, lukewarm, not hot, just as you would if she was alive and suffering from hypothermia. She was frozen through, she'll have to be warmed through. Two, three hours...shall we say three p.m. for the PM?"

"Fine." Hennessey nodded.

"You'll be attending for the police, Inspector?"

"Yes. I think so."

"Good, see you then. Ha...rectal temperature's zero...below in fact...what a surprise." She stood and covered the body with the plastic sheet. "Well, you'll be here for a while yet?"

"Sweeping the wood, yes."

"I'll proceed to York District...if you can arrange for the body to be conveyed there? I'll see you at three p.m., Chief Inspector."

Hennessey drove back to York. He had not expected the sweep of the wood to produce anything of interest and he

was not disappointed. The wood was a thick mass of vegetation; a fingertip search was out of the question. All the
officers had been able to manage was to form a line, which
rapidly became ragged, and hack away vegetation with
branches they had cut from saplings and may, thought
Hennessey, equally have trampled and covered any item of
relevance as found it. Nonetheless, the sweep had to be
done. Hennessey left Yellich and the uniformed officers to
tidy up the locus by removing the tape and set two officers
to walk the grass verge which ran between the wood and
road in search of tyre tracks, though he similarly believed it
to have been a fruitless exercise, but again, one which had
to be done. He found time to ponder that the constables
would have enjoyed it, just the day for a stroll in the country, far better than patrolling the baking streets of the city.
He reached York and inched through summer tourist-
slowed traffic to Micklegate Bar Police Station and parked
his car at the rear. Leaving one window open a few inches,
he walked across the car park to the rear Staff Only
entrance and signed in at the enquiry desk. He checked his
pigeonhole and found, with some relief, it contained just
three circulars – nothing of pressing need. He walked from
the enquiry desk to the CID corridor and to his office. He
hung his panama on the hat stand and put his jacket on the
rear of his chair. Coffee did not have an appeal on a day that
after a shower of rain had become hot, too hot for his taste,
and promised, nay threatened, Hennessey thought, threatened to become even hotter and so he put a teabag in a mug
which had 'Yorkshire' in gold letters on a blue background
and switched on the electric kettle which stood on a table
in the corner of the room. While waiting for it to boil, he
glanced out through the small window of his office and out
across Micklegate Bar to the ancient walls of the medieval
city which, at that moment, were thronged with tourists.

All nations seemed to Hennessey to be represented, Americans, easily recognised by their choice of clothing of loud colour...bright blue jackets, or yellow chequered patterns and Japanese...had to be Japanese, Hennessey thought, the only oriental nation whose citizens seem to have the freedom and the money to travel. There were olive skinned Mediterranean folk, tall, pale-skinned Europeans, all weaving in and out amongst each other as they walked in opposite directions. It was when viewing the walls carrying foot passengers in such quantity that Hennessey believed a one-way system should be imposed, yet allowing folk to weave in and out of each other's paths he had to concede, did indeed seem to work, because despite the drop on the inner side of the wall, the battlements being only on the outer aspect of the wall, there never seemed to be any incident of anyone being jostled over the edge with possible bone fracturing consequences. Above the walkers of the walls, the sky was once again clear and cloudless and the sun recommenced its relentless beating down.

The kettle boiled and Hennessey slopped the water over the teabag, added powdered milk 'not to be given to babies' and carried the steaming concoction to his desk. He sat down, and placing the mug to his right, picked up the telephone and punched a four figure internal number.

"Collator." The reply was swift, efficient, enthusiastic.

"DCI Hennessey."

"Yes, sir."

"I need a file number please, for a new case."

"Yes, sir...it would be..." Hennessey listened and heard the tapping of a computer keyboard, "it would be...it would be 30/08 of this year sir."

"Thirty!" Hennessey glanced at his watch, twelve forty.

"Yes, sir."

"But it's just past midday. We have had thirty crimes

reported since midnight?"

"Yes, sir. August has just begun and already we have had thirty crimes reported…well, your request is the thirtieth. Mostly thefts, sir, and mostly the victims have been tourists."

"Yes, rich pickings for the felons, as always."

"Indeed, sir…theft from cars has been reported on a few occasions, but it's mostly pickpocketing and lifting of cameras only put down for a few moments."

"Which is all it takes. Well, this is a murder, hope that's the only one so far."

"Indeed it is, sir…thankfully."

"Well, thank you, 30/08 of this year it is." Hennessey scribbled the number on his pad and then stood and crossed to the filing cabinet and pulled out a new file and added a dozen sheets of recording paper. He returned to his desk, added the sheets to the file and on the front of the file he wrote 30/08 and glanced at the dotted lines against the words 'name' and 'address' and pondered the details that would shortly be written on said dotted lines. He picked up the phone and jabbed another four figure internal number and listened to the soft warbling of the ringing tone, as it rang seemingly endlessly. He was about to put the phone down when it was eventually answered.

"Sorry…" a breathless voice panted in Hennessey's ear, "I was on the other line…press officer…"

"DCI Hennessey."

"Yes, sir."

"Can you prepare a press release?"

"Certainly, sir."

"Body of a young adult female found in Sparrow Wood by Stillwater Lake in the Vale of York."

"Oh…" the press officer groaned, the groan of sympathy of a sensitive man.

"Yes, methinks this will turn out to be a particularly tragic case. We have not yet established her identity, no cause of death has been found...but we are treating it as murder."

"Beyond 'suspicious' then, sir?"

"Yes...beyond suspicious...well beyond suspicious... she was naked you see, and this is the real rub...she was found to be in a deep frozen state."

"Good grief!"

"Yes. Which means we don't know when she was killed."

"Could have been years ago."

"Exactly," Hennessey allowed a note of solemnity to enter his voice, "but while she could have been kept in a frozen state for any length of time, we also believe that she was dumped in the hours of darkness last night and dumped in a hurry, as though the murderer had been startled into that action by a sudden and unexpected change in his circumstances. She was also laid out rather than folded, indicating an industrial sized deep freeze."

"I see, sir. So, you'd like to talk to any tourist who last night heard a lot of noise from the kitchen of the hotel he is staying in..." said with a glimmer of humour which Hennessey didn't think was at all callous. Such humour was necessary for anyone in any capacity of police work, so George Hennessey had found at a very early stage of his career. "Well the press will love this...headlines in the evening paper...headlines in the morning paper, lead item in the regional television and radio news."

"Just what we need," said Hennessey. "This is one of those cases where we need all the publicity we can get. Thanks."

He replaced the phone and began the recording in the file. The discovery of the body, the action taken and time the action was taken.

Hennessey closed the file and put it in the filing cabinet and locked the cabinet, Home Office Rules being Home Office Rules. He signed out at the enquiry desk as a young constable was struggling to give directions to a foreign tourist. "Left...left..." he tapped his arm, "left...second left." And the tourist, middle-aged and overweight said "Si...si...left...two left...si." Hennessey smiled to himself, he well remembered such trials and tribulations when he was a young constable.

He stepped out of the main doorway of the late Victorian building that was Micklegate Bar Police Station. A complicated design, he had always thought, typical of its day, and rendered in red brick, now darkened with soot over the hundred plus years of its existence. He stood on the pavement as the heat of the sun hit him like a blast from a suddenly opened oven door and he glanced up at Micklegate Bar where the head of Harry Hotspur had once been impaled and been left to decay for three years as a warning to any who might defy the Crown. Hennessey knew, as did all citizens of York, that the best way to cross the town is to walk the walls, but the walls at that hour being congested with tourists, he felt that he would make better progress if he kept at street level. He walked down Micklegate with its succession of pubs which he had heard had given rise to the 'Micklegate Challenge'; the attempt to have one half pint of beer in each pub: no one has ever been known to have achieved it. He crossed the Ouse at the Ouse Bridge and turned left into Spurriergate. The city thronged, the doors of the shops in Coney Street were flung wide as the air-conditioning struggled to cope, a young man with a harsh rasping voice and a limited knowledge of guitar chords busked near the entrance of a shop which seemed to be doing good business. Hennessey counted four coins in the busker's hat as he walked past.

The man's musical talents clearly made little impression on the foot passengers. Further on down Coney Street sweet classical music floated from two young women, probably university students, Hennessey guessed. Dressed for the weather in cheesecloth shirts and long cotton skirts, they played a violin duet that Hennessey, albeit with an uneducated ear for music, thought faultless. Unlike the busker, the two girls had made an impression on the passing citizenry and their collection pot, an old bowler hat, was plentiful with coin and note. Further on still, a young woman sat beneath a shop window. She had on a length of string a black-coated puppy which looked to be suffering in the heat. She held a piece of cardboard on which she had written 'homeless and hungry, please help'. Seeing the girl, Hennessey stopped at a sandwich bar and bought a packet of sandwiches in a plastic carton together with a bottle of mineral water. Leaving the shop, he approached the girl who seemed to be a waiflike thing of approximately eighteen years. Her sunken eyes told of long-term substance abuse. He opened the sandwiches and kneeling down, placed the sandwiches on her knee and poured the mineral water into the now empty carton and laid the carton in front of the puppy which had become animated at the sound of pouring water and commenced to drink desperately. "I'm a policeman." Hennessey spoke quietly, not knowing if the girl was fully receptive to him. He was aware that drug addicts and derelicts occupy a strange world of emotional detachment. Indeed the girl blinked curiously at him but otherwise showed no response, and sadly, he thought, showed no interest in the food he had placed on her knee. "I'm coming back this way in half an hour's time and if you are still here, I am going to arrest you, you hear me?" The girl still did not respond. "Begging is an offence, but more so is causing suffering to an animal. When did that dog last drink?" Still no response, but a vacant blinking. "And you're in direct sunlight. Do you know how uncomfortable dogs are in the sun, especially dark-coloured dogs? And when did you last eat? Might be a good idea to arrest you, get both you and your dog somewhere you both need to be. Hear me? Half an hour." He stood and walked on and as he did so, the words he spoke to the girl beggar ran through his mind like an unstoppable mantra. At St Helen's Square he turned right and weaved and zigzagged through the crowd and entered narrow Stonegate. In Stonegate he turned left into a snickelway, which was cool and welcoming, at the end of which covered passage was the entrance to the Starre Inn, 'York's oldest pub'. He entered the low-beamed pub and, having ordered a meal and a double soda water with a strong dash of lime, found a vacant chair and table in the corner. He sat awaiting his meal under a print of a map of 'Yorkshyrre' dated 1610, the same vintage as the pub itself he noted, and with the 'famous and faire Citie York defcribed'. Half an hour later he was fully replenished with a meal of Cumberland sausage with onion gravy. He walked slowly out of the pub, allowing his meal to settle, and braced himself to meet the heat of the sun as he exited the snickelway. Once again, in the crowd of gently walking, elderly and dashing children who didn't seem to feel the heat, he retraced his steps, and mindful of advice once given to his class at the Trafalgar Road School by their teacher, to wit 'never make an idle threat', he strolled into Coney Street. The young beggar girl and her black mongrel were nowhere to be seen.

He walked back up winding Micklegate, the slight incline proving something of an obstacle in the heat. He entered the cool interior of Micklegate Bar Police Station and was greeted with a cheery 'afternoon, sir' by the constable at the enquiry desk.

"Afternoon. Did you help the gentleman?"

"Which? Oh, the Italian? Yes I think so, sir...*si, si*, this is left...*si*..." The constable grinned. "Mind, I shouldn't laugh, he spoke better English than I can speak Italian. Anyway, he hasn't come back so I think he found what he was looking for, being the Railway museum."

"Be hot in there today." Hennessey thought of the huge canopy that was the National Railway Museum. "Like being in a greenhouse."

"High roof, sir, probably be alright."

"Yes..." He replied absentmindedly as he checked his pigeonhole. There were more circulars, but again, thankfully, nothing of pressing need. He walked into the CID corridor and, glancing into Somerled Yellich's office, saw Yellich at his desk, jacket slung over his chair, sleeves rolled up. He stood in the doorway. "Sweep reveal anything?"

"Not a thing, boss...didn't think it would...that foliage could swallow anything. But at least we did it."

"I've notified the press officer, full press release will be made. I'm going to have the deceased photographed. I'll ask for an e-fit to be composed, should be about the most accurate e-fit ever."

"Blimey, yes." Yellich raised his eyebrows. "Next best thing to releasing the actual photograph."

"Yes, ought to be able to let the press have the e-fit tomorrow...at least in time for the evening papers and evening television. If she was local, we should get a response. The crime is definitely local...but she could be Australian..."

"Yes...I had thought of that." Yellich patted the cases on his desk. "Well, I'm just catching up on a few loose ends. I get the feeling the lady in the woods is going to occupy both our time over the next day or two."

"I am of like mind, Yellich. I'll be at York City this afternoon." He glanced at his watch. "In fact I'd better cut along there now. Traffic will be heavy, in fact it is heavy."

"Not walking, skipper? Not like you to drive."

"Too hot to walk, Yellich. I've just walked out for lunch. The car's got a fan."

Hennessey drove the short distance from Micklegate Bar Police Station to York District Hospital. The traffic, as he had previously observed it to be, was slow and heavy but the window wound fully down and the fan on as cool as it could be set, combined to make the journey bearable, but only just, for beads of sweat trickled from his scalp. He parked his car in the car park of the hospital and as he walked towards the medium-rise slab-sided building, he looked about him for that car, a certain distinct vehicle, and located it in the area reserved for 'Doctors' Parking', a red and white Riley RMA circa 1949...over fifty years old...still sitting solidly on its suspension, still gleaming in the sun. He smiled as he saw it, and let his eyesight linger over it, not looking where he was going for a few safe paces. He entered the hospital, welcomed by a chill body of cool conditioned air that he found refreshing after the heat. Once in the hospital, he walked a familiar route to the pathology laboratory. Moments later he sat in Dr Louise D'Acre's cramped office. Displayed proudly throughout were photographs of pre-teen, and teenage children, a boy and two girls respectively. A sturdy looking horse also figured predominantly in the photographs.

"The body has been thawed," she said, after inviting Hennessey to sit. "We are ready to commence the postmortem."

"I'd like to have photographs taken of the head and face, for our purposes. I want to give them to our artist, he can build up an e-fit or CD fit as they are now called."

"Technology makes its relentless progress." Dr D'Acre had a soft voice, a serious manner, but Hennessey had always found warmth in her eyes.

"Indeed. Identi-fits gave way to e-fits. I still use that term...now it's CD fit. But from a photograph of the face, our artist can create a very accurate likeness for a CD fit which we can release to the press."

"Yes, I am sure Mr Filey will be able to accommodate you there. If he puts his mind to it, he might be able to get the prints over to you today. He's a good man and we are lucky to have him but he can be a bit of a clock-watcher...claims for every bit of overtime beyond thirty minutes and likes to down tools at five if he can. If he's got time, he'll print the photographs for you today...just to warn you he might make you wait until tomorrow."

"Tomorrow would do." Hennessey leaned forward. "If we could have them in the morning, we could produce the CD fit by the evening, if not the lunchtime news."

"Good...there will be no name yet, I imagine?"

"Not yet. So far she is case 30/08 of this year."

Louise D'Acre glanced at him, held eye contact, a very rare thing for her to do, and raised an eyebrow.

"Yes," Hennessey nodded, "I commented as much to our collator. The tourists make easy pickings, 29 cases of cameras and such being stolen and this...the murder of she who is still to be named."

"Well, if you'd like to change and scrub, we'll try to let Mr Filey have some time."

Hennessey walked to the male changing rooms, stripped to his underwear, scrubbed his hands and face and clambered into green paper disposable coveralls and then slipped on matching footwear.

Eric Filey was already in the pathology laboratory when

Hennessey entered and took up his customary position against the wall, observing for the police but not closing the actual dissection table unless invited, as dictated by both procedure and protocol. Filey was a short, rotund man and most often, in Hennessey's experience, was possessed of a jovial, eager attitude and he had been a little saddened to hear that the man was a 'bit of a clock-watcher'. Filey smiled and nodded at Hennessey who returned the compliment. Hennessey glanced around him. He had been in this laboratory many, many times before, so many times, he had come to think that he could find his way round the room blindfolded. There was the bench which ran along the further wall of the rectangular room with drawers which contained instruments, sample jars, production sachets, cupboards above the bench which contained less heavy equipment; towels, wipes, a few text books. In the centre of the room were four stainless steel tables set at an equal distance from each other and set in a row. Each table had a lip round the edge to contain any blood that might spill from a corpse, and each table was supported by a single pedestal in which ran a waste pipe to allow any such blood to drain away. Only one of the tables was occupied, the second from the left, in front of which Hennessey had placed himself. On that table lay the body of the young female which earlier that day had been stumbled across by a harmless soul seeking only to obtain an uninterrupted view of a pair of red kites. She lay wraithlike in her paleness, while even in a room, the predominant colour of which was white, even the relentless glow of the filament bulbs in the ceiling shielded behind sheets of opaque Perspex, could not bring any semblance of colour to her face. She lay there, so cruelly robbed of life when still of few years, so fortunately attractive, which, as he had earlier commented, may have led to her downfall, now lifeless, save for a starched white towel placed over her coyly termed 'private parts'. Eric Filey and Hennessey realised that they were both looking at the body, then looked at each other across the disinfectant scented room and seemed to know what they were both thinking.

"There's no justice in life." Eric Filey spoke for both of them. "No justice at all, or fairness…no fairness about it at all."

"None," Hennessey grimaced. "None."

Dr D'Acre entered the room and any conversation which might have developed between Hennessey and the pathology assistant was instantly and reverentially stifled.

"Afternoon, gentlemen."

"Ma'am," Filey nodded.

"Dr D'Acre," Hennessey added, even though he and she had met briefly a few moments beforehand, the formality and gravity of a post-mortem had to be observed.

"Mr Filey, can we please have photographs of the deceased, particularly the head and face."

"Yes, ma'am." Eric Filey reached for a 35mm camera with a flash attachment and took a series of photographs of the deceased's head and face.

"Can you copy those to the police as soon as you can, please, Mr Filey?"

"Yes, ma'am."

"They're needed to produce a CD fit."

"Understood, ma'am." Filey placed the camera gently on the bench.

Dr D'Acre adjusted the position of the microphone attached to the end of a stainless steel anglepoise which protruded from the ceiling above the dissecting table. "This is my reference L/D1/61F of this year and police reference 30/08 of this year," said clearly for the benefit of an audio typist. Dr D'Acre considered the corpse. "The body is that of a north west European or Caucasian of the female sex.

She is approximately twenty years of age and is well nourished. Her identity is as yet unknown. The body measures..." She stretched a metal tape measure from the top of the skull to the feet, "just five feet tall...or 1.5 metres, approximately. Slender. Blonde hair. There are no discernible injuries to the anterior of the body. The body was found in a frozen condition...put that before the last sentence, please. Mr Filey...if you could hold the feet...we'll be turning clockwise from your aspect." Filey moved to the foot of the table and took hold of the deceased's feet as Dr D'Acre said, "Three, two, one..." And the corpse was efficiently flipped over onto its stomach. "There are similarly no discernible injuries to the posterior...once again, Mr Filey...three, two, one." And the body was once again laid face up on the table and, without prompting, Eric Filey placed the white towel over the genitalia.

"Thank you, Mr Filey. The limbs are flaccid, having thawed for a few hours, and I will expect the blood to recover some of its fluidity. There is a notable absence of hypostasis." She turned to Hennessey, "Lividity caused by the settling of blood...after the heart stops, the blood retains a fluidity and will settle according to gravity and will congeal there, causing a purple discoloration of the skin, very noticeable in white and Latin peoples...more difficult to detect in Asian and Afro-Caribbean peoples...but in this case, it's absent...totally. There is no indication that blood has been drained from the body...the lacerations would be evident if it had...so, she was frozen immediately, almost immediately after death and the blood froze in her veins and arteries before it could settle. The other grim alternative..." again she glanced at Hennessey, "is that she was placed in the freezer while alive and she froze to death."

"Grim," Hennessey responded, "as you say."

"Especially if she was conscious. Not so bad if she was

unconscious and didn't know what was happening...but bad enough still."

"Indeed." Hennessey pondered the fear, the terror, of knowing one was freezing to death.

"Hello..." Dr D'Acre felt the scalp of the deceased. "There is a lump on the rear of the head, a distinct mound...probably an injury...a bang on the head could have caused a loss of consciousness...there is a raised area on the posterior aspect of the skull about ten centimetres across. It's linear, the sort of injury that would be caused by falling against a hard edge, or by a linear object being brought with force against the skull." Dr D'Acre paused. "It's of some significance...it's contemporary with her death...this corpse having been frozen is like a time capsule, and this lump meant she may, mercifully, have been unconscious when frozen. I would like to think so for her sake." Dr D'Acre placed one hand on the deceased's jaw and held the head with her other hand. She moved the jaw from one side to the other and then pulled the jaw downwards and peered into the mouth. "Well, I never..."

"Something?" Hennessey asked, forgetting himself. The unwritten rules did not permit observing police officers to comment or question during a post-mortem. Speak when spoken to and approach the dissecting table only if, and when, invited being the dictat.

"Nope..." Dr D'Acre clearly allowed the question. "Nothing...except perfect teeth. It is remarkable. I have never, in all my years, come across anybody who has achieved this age and not had dental treatment. It really is quite remarkable...the teeth are not neglected...I don't mean that, they are perfect...no treatment has been required." She stood upright and turned to Hennessey. "The only time I ever heard of a young adult being observed with perfect teeth was from a friend of mine who is in general practice in the south of England. She had occasion once to see a young woman who presented to her surgery with a throat infection...looked into her mouth with a spatula, 'Say, ah...', you know the form..."

"Yes...certainly do."

"The patient had a throat which was raw with inflammation but what Doreen...my friend...what Doreen found remarkable where her teeth. Absolutely perfect. Turned out that the patient was an exchange student, from the Soviet Union as it then was, had grown up with a sugar free diet." She tapped the forehead of the corpse with her fingertip. "Perhaps that's what you have here...even my son, aged ten, has teeth which would be put to shame by these teeth."

"It'll be worth following up," Hennessey conceded. "It's a very interesting point."

"We'll, I am loath to look at the brain...that would mean removing the skin from the face and head...the lump is not serious enough to cause brain injury and speaks for a good, thick skull...not an eggshell skull, so called. We can recommence the PM if we need to look inside her head. Let's look inside the stomach." Dr D'Acre took the scalpel and drew it across the stomach, opened the cavity and peered inside. "Well, she died very shortly after eating a meal...still frozen for us: meat; vegetables; what looks like sponge pudding; home cooking...could be a restaurant, but for food to be in this state when frozen, it means she must have been placed in the freezer within an hour of finishing the last course. The freezing has captured the state of her body at the moment of her death, it may in fact be the cause of it. It was possibly during the winter months...the sponge pudding, you see...just an observation thrown in."

"Throw all you like...please." Hennessey smiled warmly.

"We'll take a blood sample. Hypodermic, please, Mr

Filey. The body is thawing out. If she was frozen before the blood congealed, it will become fluid as it thaws before congealing and any light poisons will be present." Dr D'Acre put the hypodermic against a vein, punctured the skin and depressed the plunger. "Do this to a live patient and you'd have to warn them about feeling a small prick...it's one of the reasons I appreciate this post, my patients don't feel pain...won't report me to the BMA...I am never worried about giving the right treatment." She withdrew the plunger, filling the hypodermic with blood. "Not as fluid as I would have thought, or liked...beginning to congeal, but enough there to send to the lab. If there's any intoxicant there, they'll find it." She handed the syringe to Eric Filey who dropped it into a production bag and labelled it. She took the towel from the genitalia and parted the legs of the corpse. "Well..." she said, examining the body, "she was sexually active, but no signs of trauma at the time she died. She wasn't a victim of rape. I'll swab for semen, I dare say that would be useful for you, Chief Inspector."

"Very," Hennessey responded, sounding interested, enthusiastic.

"If it's there...but it appears not. I'll swab anyway. Swabs please, Mr Filey."

The swab produced, a vaginal smear was taken and the swab, like the syringe, similarly placed in a production bag and labelled.

"A blow to the back of the head." Dr D'Acre replaced the towel. "Insufficient to kill her...could have rendered her unconscious, whereupon she was frozen. You know, freezing someone to death is about the only form of murder that I can think of which will not leave any injuries, or any clues as to the cause of death. If she hadn't been found, had thawed out and begun to decompose, it would have been quite a mystery. As it is...good luck for you and me, bad luck for the culprit."

"No culprit yet…but yes, when we find him or her, it was bad luck that a man picked his way through that wood, a few feet either side and he would have missed her. It was as thickly foliaged as a tropical rainforest in there."

"Yes, I know what you mean." Dr D'Acre smiled as she rescued Hennessey from his fumbling. "Good luck/ bad luck depending on your standpoint. And her last meal, a heavy winter meal. The teeth…she just could not have achieved her years with perfect dentures had she lived in the West with its sugar-rich diet."

"It's a real pointer," Hennessey conceded. He glanced at his watch. "Might just be able to contact the university before they draw stumps for the day."

"This is an incomplete post-mortem, Chief Inspector, but it's as far as I want to take it, which is the other advantage of this type of patient, you can halt the operation halfway through and put him or her back in a drawer, pick up the operation at a later date. There's no reason for me to cut her head open. I could remove a tooth to obtain her age at death, plus or minus one year, but her face is so perfectly preserved that if she has been reported missing there ought to be a photograph of her, and confirmation can be had by DNA matching. At this age, she is likely to have living relatives."

"Understood."

"Cause of death cannot be determined but likely to be hypothermia. I'll fax my report to you as soon as it's typed…be some time tomorrow."

"Thanks, I appreciate it."

Hennessey changed back into his clothing disposing of the coveralls in a "sin bin" from where they would be taken to the hospital incinerator. He walked out of the changing rooms, along the silent, solemn corridors of the hospital and out into the car park. Four-thirty...the sun was still high and harsh and a heat haze shimmered above the tarmac of the car park. He drove a slow, halting journey through the streets of the ancient city. The traffic already heavy by then, had been aggravated by the beginning of the rush hour. It was past five when he finally turned into the car park of Micklegate Bar Police Station. At his desk he picked up the phone and dialled the university and asked to be put through to the Department of Modern Languages. A helpful porter with a warm south of England accent advised Hennessey that all the staff "'ave gone 'ome." Then he added a little needlessly for Hennessey's taste. "Be 'ere tomorrow though, governor." Hennessey thanked him and replaced the phone. He was in no hurry to return to his "'ome" and so took the file marked '30/08' from the filing cabinet and recorded Dr D'Acre's initial observations and possible cause of death and that the deceased may well be of Eastern European origin. He wrote slowly, killing time, allowing the rush hour to subside. Being bumper to bumper in that heat was an experience he could well live without. He picked up the phone and dialled a four figure internal number.

"Collator." The reply was again brisk, efficient.

"DCI Hennessey."

"Yes, sir."

"Female"

"Yes, sir."

"Late teens, early twenties?"

"Yes, sir."

"Possibly east European?"

"East European? Not many of those."

"Yes...extend that to include the Soviet Union as was, Federation of Russian States as is now."

"Yes, sir."

"Blonde hair…slender of build. Just five feet tall…about 1.5 metres."

"Yes, sir."

"No distinguishing features."

"Very good, sir."

"Enter that into your box of tricks, see if you get a result with respect to any missing persons that have been reported to us."

"Very good, sir."

"If no local result, send that down to the National Missing Person's Helpline in London, see if they can match if up."

"Yes, sir."

"Thanks." Hennessey replaced the phone. He collected his jacket and walked to the canteen. The bar was open, police officers in white shirts had unhooked their ties and sat drinking casually, darts thudded into a full size cork dartboard which had been kept in water overnight as all dartboards should be and still glistened with moisture. A television set high on the wall was tuned into the sports channel with the sound mercifully kept down. Hennessey bought a soda water and lime and selected a *Yorkshire Post* and the *Guardian* from the newspaper rack. It was, he had found, as pleasant a way to unwind after a busy day as could be had. At six p.m., the rush hour having subsided, he drove home in a cool evening to a warm house.

Chapter Two

Friday, 2nd of August – 08.30 hours
in which Yellich visits the university and an elderly man feeds a young girl.

George Hennessey sat at his desk, shirt sleeves rolled up military style, cuff over cuff, looking at the photographs of the deceased which had arrived by courier, received at 18.40hrs the previous day according to the note. So perhaps the jovial Eric Filey was not such a clock-watcher after all? There were six photographs, all perfectly focused, all black and white, being much better for defining facial features than colour film. One photograph seemed to have been printed twice and so he removed it and stapled it to the inside of the file. The remaining prints he put in an internal mail envelope and addressed it to the police artist, adding a note requesting they be used for the basis of a CD fit and returned for his attention asap. That sent off, he turned his attention to the report from the collator following his request of the previous day.

"Svetlana Zvonoreva," he read aloud, and then read on silently, nineteen years, of St Petersburg, formerly Leningrad, a language student, reported missing, December 19th, three years ago. He compared the photograph in the missing persons file to the photograph taken by Eric Filey. One photograph showed a young woman wide-eyed with the joy of youth and excitement of being in the West, the other showed a lifeless face with eyes closed. Of huge, of monumental importance though was that the photographs appeared to be of the same young woman. He stood and carried the two photographs to Yellich's office. He tapped on the doorframe as he entered.

"Morning, skipper." Yellich looked up from his desk, as Hennessey entered and smiled a radiant smile.

"Morning, Yellich. Have a look at these photographs, tell me what you think." He handed the two prints to Yellich.

"Well..." Yellich held a print in each hand and glanced from one to the other three or four times, "they're very similar. I recognise the dissecting table at the pathology laboratory. Eric Filey must have stood on a chair to get that shot."

"Yes, clearly did it after the PM, quite conscientious of him, and in no small contrast to what Dr D'Acre told me about him."

"Oh?"

"Yes, not important, but I think close enough to assume it's a match."

"Yes... I'd be prepared to run with it, boss. One photograph could be superimposed on the other, that would prove it one way or another if the eye orbits perfectly align and the mouth and nose too."

"Yes, DNA would be another way of doing it but I'm loathe to ask Interpol to ask her parents for a lock of hair each, I'd rather contact them with bad news or not at all."

"Yes, boss."

"What are you doing?"

"As yesterday boss, catching up on paperwork and I've got that report to complete on Hawkins and son."

"Who are they?"

"Father and son serial burglary team. The Crown Prosecution Service wants it yesterday."

"Well they can wait. I want you to give this priority."

"Very good, boss." Yellich closed the file in which he had been writing.

"The name of the missing person who may have been

the selfsame person found in a deep frozen condition yesterday forenoon was Svetlana Zvonoreva, Russian, from St Petersburg."

"I was going to ask."

"Dr D'Acre did mention the possibility of her being of Eastern European descent."

"Really? Looks, well...could be any nationality reality, in fact she looks like a Scots lass I knew once, though I don't mean in the Biblical sense...not for want of trying though. Before I was wed, I hasten to add."

"I never thought any other," Hennessey smiled. "The reason – you can't see it on the photograph – but she has perfect teeth. I mean not perfectly formed, but perfectly preserved."

"No dental work at all?"

"No, not needed. She had lived with a sugar-free diet, so Dr D'Acre advised. Only in Eastern Europe and the Russian Federation would people of that ethnic group, Northern Europeans, live with a sugar free diet."

"Clever of her."

"Experience, really, she'd seen it before, or rather a friend of hers had, she said. I like that about her, she could have claimed a deductive process, but was honest enough to admit to having heard about such before. A lesser pathologist might not even have commented on the perfect state of her teeth, nothing damaged so nothing to investigate. But Dr D'Acre puts us on course."

"Yes, I think we are very lucky to have her."

"Well Svetlana's last address was care of the Dept. of Modern Languages at the university."

Yellich stood and reached for his jacket, suitably lightweight, Hennessey noted. "I'll start there and see where I get to."

"Which is all you can do."

Yellich wrote her name in his notebook and asked how old she was. Hennessey told him, and Yellich sighed as he added nineteen under her name.

Yellich drove out to Heslington, the modern and already well-established university, brick built teaching and accommodation blocks and bars, and food halls and sports facilities on a landscaped greenfield site complete with a small, relaxing lake within the campus. It was, he had heard, the sort of university where hopeful students visit and think, "I've just got to come here," with its cloistered atmosphere of seclusion, but once at the university, said student discovers the closed and trapped feeling that is a campus university and soon yearns for 'real life' outside and drinks in the city and rents accommodation off campus. Yellich walked the winding pathway beside the small lake, on which ducks swam, other ducks content to sit on the grass amongst the flower beds. Two students, he very handsome, she very beautiful, walked towards him arm in arm. They looked at him as they approached and then looked past him when they were about six feet away, clearly dismissing him by his appearance as one of a lesser social status. Another female student ran past him, jogging with headset attached to a CD player. A bearded student sat on the grass, reading a textbook and nodded at Yellich as they glanced at each other. Above, the sky was broad and near cloudless, scarred, it seemed to Yellich, by the vapour trail of an overhead airliner. And above all was the sun, high and relentless. Even after the short walk from the car park to the Dept. of Modern Languages, Yellich found great relief to be out of the sun in a pleasantly air-conditioned environment.

"Oh, no. Oh no." The woman seemed to Yellich to be genuine in her sorrow and distress. "But after this time there would be no hope of her returning unharmed, even if still alive. Dead, you say...oh dear."

"The body was found in the wood by Stillwater Lake. It was in the news last night."

"That was Svetlana!"

"We believe so. Still to be confirmed, but the frozen nature of the body meant that it had been preserved."

"Of course."

"The photographs of the deceased match the photograph of Svetlana on the mis per report...hair colour... height...all matched. It will be quite remarkable if it isn't her. Everything points to it being Svetlana Zvonoreva."

"It seems so." Felicity Doubleday PhD, by the nameplate on her desk, sat back in her chair. "So how may I help you, Mr...?"

"Yellich."

"Yellich? That's an Eastern European name, not intact...has been corrupted...lost its integrity along the way. Slavic I would have thought...possibly. Do you know its origin?"

"No, we don't, but my ancestors were believed to be refugees."

"Ah...well, how may I help?" Felicity Doubleday was dark-haired, soberly dressed in green, Yellich found her to have a warm smile, a warm manner...peaceful doe eyes. She was, he thought, of that ilk of which he understood to be referred to as a 'woman's woman'.

"Well, Svetlana Zvonoreva, nineteen years old when she was reported missing, anything you can tell us about her?"

"Yes...a quiet young woman, excited about being in the West but I think she found it daunting. She was with us on a one year – that is a one academic year. Exchange course...October to June...a good student, keen to learn, she was studying English in Russia but came to this department as a conversation facilitator. She helped our students master Russian, improved their grasp of the language and in turn we gave tuition in English. We had French and Spanish students at the same time but she was the only student from Eastern Europe that year. I don't think she was relishing the prospect of returning to Russia. That's a problem that many Eastern Bloc students have but there is a lot of pressure on them to return. Even in these post-Soviet days the state can make things difficult for their families and if too many try to overstay their visa then the Russian students after them will probably be prevented from having the opportunity to live and study in the West. They are told that. The Russian culture has developed to make individuals feel guilty for letting the state and fellow citizens down...thanks to Communism...and so the great majority return."

"The great majority?"

"Well, we haven't had any student jump ship, as it were, when their time came to return to Mother Russia...gone into hiding...flown to the States...turned their backs on family and country. That has never happened but one or two women over the years have married Englishmen though I confess I am suspect of the sincerity of the relationship when I have met one or two of the husbands...overweight, balding men with their 'trophy wives' who are attractive enough to model swimwear and youthful enough to be their daughters. But it's a price Russian female students have been known to pay in order to remain in the West and as a means of staying it is particularly attractive because it is not seen as a betrayal of trust. The Russians value the institution of marriage and as such, marriage to a westerner met during the exchange period is an acceptable reason in the eyes of the state for not returning home and the girls' families will not be persecuted."

"I see." Yellich glanced at the wall of Felicity Doubleday's office, posters of Moscow and Leningrad, and framed photographs of herself with brutal looking housing in the background. "You know Russia?"

"Yes, I think so. I have visited a number of times and was an exchange teacher for a while. Lovely people, very generous spirited. I have little time for Communism as a political ideal, frankly it just didn't work, but Russian culture gave the world Chekhov and Tolstoy...well, the list goes on."

"Yes."

"It was Communism, not Russian culture, that gave the world Chernobyl and the destruction of the Aral Sea ecosystem."

"I understand the distinction, but we are moving away from Svetlana Zvonoreva."

"Yes we are. I think she was husband hunting...specifically western husband hunting. The majority of girls come to university with an elephant gun slung over one shoulder with which they hope to bag a husband, but Svetlana was also looking for the passport."

"She was seeing someone?"

"That I don't know." Felicity Doubleday pursed her lips. "I am trying to think who might. The problem is, you see, that she was part of a transitory population, being the undergraduates, it will be difficult to trace her friends as it was three years ago." She reached for the phone on her desk. "Excuse me," she smiled as she spoke and dialled an internal number. "Hello, Felicity Doubleday, is that Carolyn? Can I talk to her, please?"

Yellich glanced at the window of Felicity Doubleday's study, the lake looked cool and inviting, the clock on the tower read 10.35. The day was going to get hotter. Yellich knew that in an hour or two, the lake would be full of fully clothed or not so fully clothed undergraduates and he felt a pang of sorrow that his own son would never experience the playing of such high jinks, never know such youthful exuberance.

"Carolyn...Felicity. Can you access the files and find Svetlana Zvonoreva's address in York? Yes, the Russian girl who disappeared. Yes, I'll hold." Felicity Doubleday glanced at Yellich and slipped her hand over the mouth-piece. "She's well remembered, at least her disappearance is, as it would be."

"Yes."

"We thought she might have defected, wrong word but you know what I mean, but she disappeared too early in the course. Arrived in the October, and if I recall, disappeared the following December."

"That's correct."

"Just before Christmas, I think."

"Not a good Christmas for her family," Yellich pondered aloud. "Hope we can at least return the body to bury, having some sort of closure to it all."

"Yes? Oh yes..." Felicity Doubleday picked up a pen and wrote as she listened. "Thank you." She replaced the receiver. "Yes, two months into her course is too early to 'defect'. Any defections I have known, not from this university but others, all seem to take place just before the end of the course, as I said. So Svetlana's disappearance was instantly suspicious." She handed Yellich a sheet of paper. "Name and address of Svetlana's landlady whilst she was here."

"Jayne Style," Yellich read, "14, The Croft, Heslington."

"A pleasant ten minute stroll from here."

It was, Yellich found, an uncomfortably hot twenty-five

minute stroll from the air-conditioned cubicle which was
Felicity Doubleday's neatly kept study to The Croft, number 14, being the home of Jayne Style.

"Yes, I remember Svetlana, I remember her well." Jayne
Style had revealed herself to be a slender lady of late middle
years. Her home, Yellich saw, was cluttered but in a soft,
feminine way with Lowry prints on the wall and a small
family of wooden hippopotamuses, each about three inches
high, which marched sedately across the mantelpiece. A
sheepskin rug lay in front of the fireplace and scatter cushions lay in between the armchairs. A copy of *Country
Walking* lay on the glass-topped coffee table. "I remember
her, not because she disappeared, but because of her personality...very bright, very sparky...she was thrilled at
being in the West but beyond that, Svetlana was a delightful
young woman. I rapidly formed the opinion that it would
be a lucky man who won her as his wife, and I don't think
the word 'won' is inappropriate. She was spoiled for choice,
but that didn't spoil her." Jayne Style wore a blue trouser
suit of light cotton. It seemed to Yellich to be very cool and
would, he thought, be quite comfortable in that heat. She
wore a wooden necklace, which seemed to say 'African
craft' but wore no other decoration, no bracelets, no rings
on her fingers, no watch.

"Any particular friend, associate?"

"Of Svetlana's? I never met any male friend. I don't
allow men in the house...I had an unfortunate experience
once with a male tenant who became too familiar. After
that, I let rooms only to foreign students and females only."

"No male visitors?"

"Nope," Jayne Style smiled. "Not one...once bitten,
you see."

"Yes, I can understand."

"But the girls come and go as they please, stay out all

night if they wish, I make no moral condemnation of their lifestyle…just a strict, no men, rule."

"I understand."

"Many are very hard working, I have been enormously impressed."

"Did Svetlana make any noise about staying in the West?"

Jayne Style pursed her lips and moved her head from side to side. "Well, I had been accommodating foreign students for only about two years up to that point…not all from the Eastern Bloc. I mention that because the answer to your question is 'yes'. Yes, she did and alarmingly early in her stay by comparison to the other Easterners I have met. Many start looking for ways to stay in the West in their third and final term."

"But not Svetlana?"

"Nope, she was looking for Mr (British) Right, from the start."

"Her tutor said pretty much the same thing but she was unable to provide a name of any friend."

"As indeed I am, Mr Yellich."

"Did she mention anybody at all?"

"Not to me. I wonder if she mentioned anything to Mary Wilson?"

"Mary Wilson?"

"Yes. Mary was an American girl; she had a room here at the same time as Svetlana. I can accommodate three students at any one time, you see."

"I see."

"And she and Svetlana got on like a house on fire. They once shared a bottle of wine, opened it at about three p.m. one Saturday and they were still talking at eight p.m. Five hours continuous natter…just the two of them. I once did something similar and it amused my husband – I am a divorcee – it amused him that women could find enough to talk about to keep them chatting away for five or six hours. But that's women, although you can only do that with someone you really click with. You really have to be on the same wavelength with someone to talk away for that length of time."

Yellich wrote 'Mary Wilson' in his notebook. "She'll be back in the States I presume? We could contact her by Interpol, ask the American police to interview her."

"Probably, but I don't think you need to, she's still in York."

"She is?"

"She is." Jayne Style smiled. "She clearly took a shine to the 'famous and faire' and upon completing her degree at Brown University, she negotiated a place back at York to do her PhD. She's a historian. Most of the girls who stay here are language students, but Mary was a historian.

Yellich smiled. "That sounds a profitable line of inquiry. What did you do with her things?"

"Kept them."

Yellich raised his eyebrows. "You still have them?"

"I still have them, but don't raise your hopes, it's mostly clothing, a few textbooks and essays."

"No address book or diary?"

"We can see. I cleared her room when it was certain she had disappeared but was loath to throw her belongings out, she had so little compared to western girls that stay with me, so I bundled them into a plastic bag...just one black plastic bin liner swallowed her possessions, and that included her top coat and footwear. She hadn't got much. I put it in the crawl space." Jayne Style pointed to the varnished floorboards. "It's beneath where you are sitting."

Access to the crawl space was via a trap door situated by the front door. Yellich, in deference to Jayne Style's age, volunteered, through somewhat gritted teeth, to lower himself into the crawl space to retrieve the black bin liner in question. It was also, he reminded himself, good police work anyway: it is good to seize the opportunity to look round a person's house, to familiarise himself of the layout of the house and this opportunity served to provide the police with the knowledge that the houses in The Croft do not have cellars. It was information which might be useful in some later inquiry. Yellich crawled a few feet in the confined space, feeling very uncomfortable as the dust ate its way into the smallest folds of his clothing. He foraged among many similar bags, each labelled where they had been tied, until he found a bag labelled 'Svetlana Z'. He turned and dragged the bin liner behind him back to the trap door.

"It's a bit dirty down there." Jayne Style stood by the trap door as Yellich pushed the bin liner out in front of him.

"Aye," he growled as he levered himself out of the hole. "You've got quite a bit of stuff down there."

"All my valuables and things of personal value, like photographs. As you get older photographs become very important to you. I put them down there because they're safer in the event of fire and burglary. A burglar isn't going to go rooting round the crawl space in search of my grandfather's watch, and fire will burn upwards, Heslington doesn't flood, so I don't fear water damage."

Yellich felt obliged to concede that her thinking was logically defensible. He began to brush himself down only to be invited by Mrs Style to 'do that outside, please'.

Back inside the house, Yellich undid the single knot at the top of the bin liner and removed the contents, one item at a time. There was, he felt, no small amount of poignancy in the exercise, not simply because they were the items of clothing of a young woman with much to live for and hoping for a new life in the West, but also because, by western standards she was evidently not a wealthy woman. The clothing was threadbare, the shoes roughly sewn and uncomfortable looking, the jewellery inexpensive and with plastic imitation rocks. A notebook was written wholly in cyrillic script and seemed to be an address book. He glanced at Jayne Style. "Do you speak or read Russian by any chance?"

"By no chance I do not." Jayne Style sat in the armchair observing Yellich. "It shouldn't be too difficult to have it translated."

"Shouldn't really." Yellich laid the notebook on one side. "It seems to be an address book, most entries seem to be foreign addresses in a Russian language. I would have thought any in the UK would be in English," Yellich flicked through the book, "and it will be the English addresses which will be relevant." He closed the book. "I'll go over that with more care at the station." Yellich delved further into the bin liner and found a watch, again inexpensive looking and plastic bangles...plastic...at her age. He thought of the young woman dressed in clothing like that, decorating herself with clearly inferior jewellery...and living in a house like this...it must have seemed like a palace to her. He had once read of housing conditions in the Soviet Union with its dreadful overcrowding; little wonder, he thought, the young and excited Svetlana Zvonoreva was seeking a British man to marry. He removed a half eaten packet of mouldy peanuts from the bin liner. He held them up and looked at Jayne Style questioningly. "You saved a packet of peanuts? It's the sort of thing that police remove when cleaning the accommodation of a deceased person. Everything, everything has to be removed, worn down toothbrushes...everything, in case a long lost relative comes out of the woodwork...we can say we removed everything from the house. If we leave anything, we can be accused of overlooking something and if that person was believed to be in possession of an item of value which has disappeared..."

"It could make things awkward for the police," Jayne Style finished the sentence for Yellich.

"Yes, it could, and why we would remove everything that isn't a fixture or a fitting, but for you to remove a half eaten bag of nuts..."

"I thought it very..." she shrugged, a fly appeared as if from nowhere and began to buzz angrily against the window, "telling, that's not the word but it's the best I can manage...very telling...to save a half eaten bag of peanuts after a night in the pub as if saving something precious, actually attaching so much importance to it that she brings it home carefully wrapped up. I thought it the act of someone who was used to food shortages. On that basis I though it churlish to throw them away."

Yellich felt the packet. "Did you open it?"

"No, I had no reason to, I was also in a bit of a hurry when I cleared her room. I was letting it to a Brazilian girl who arrived early."

"I see." Yellich unwound the foil. "There's more than peanuts in here." He opened the bag and glanced inside. "Well, well..."

"What is it?" Jayne Style leaned forward. "I feel bad that I missed something."

"You were not looking for anything," Yellich smiled at her, "but the important thing is that you didn't throw it away."

'It' revealed itself to be a disposable cigarette lighter, which Yellich held gingerly by the mechanism at the top. He read the logo on the side. "Liaisons, something...Long Close Lane, York...mean anything to you?"

"Not a thing." Jayne Style reached for the telephone directory and turned to the business section.

"It's a bit faded with use but it looks like 132 Long Close Lane."

"Doesn't matter anyway, there's no listing. This directory is about twelve months old, so whatever it was, it went out of business before this directory was printed."

"Thanks." Yellich placed the lighter inside a production bag and placed the bag of peanuts in another similar bag.

"You're saving the peanuts?" Jayne Style was intrigued.

"It may have latents on it, on the bag...not the peanuts."

"Latents?"

"Fingerprints."

"After this length of time?"

"After this length of time inside a plastic bin liner, yes. Why not?"

Yellich looked into the bin liner feeling a bit like a child on Christmas day morning. A few more items of clothing were extracted, examined and laid on one side before he found a book of matches, black, glossy black, with the logo 'Duck and Drake' embossed in white on the front, and a phone number beneath. He opened the book, half the matches remained and on the inside flap in a round purposeful hand was written 'Leo' and a phone number. Yellich showed the hand writing to Jayne Style. "Recognise it?"

"It's Svetlana's." She spoke with certainty, with self-assuredness. "Definitely. Check with the address book."

Yellich did. "Yes, same handwriting alright." He placed the book of matches in a production bag. "I want to keep hold of the address book, the book of matches and the lighter..."

"Fine by me. If you could jot me a receipt, just to keep us both right."

"Yes." Yellich put the clothing back in the plastic bin

liner and propped it against the side of the settee. He hand-wrote a receipt on a page of his notebook, tore it out and handed it to Jayne Style. He stood to leave. "Thank you for your co-operation," he smiled, "I appreciate it." Jayne Style looked puzzled, stone faced. "You're not leaving without putting the bin liner back in the crawl space, are you, young man?"

The phone on Hennessey's desk rang, in a soft, warbling tone. He let it ring twice and then picked it up. "DCI Hennessey."

"Switchboard, sir, forensic lab at Wetherby for you."

"Put them through, please."

The line clicked.

"Forensic laboratory at Wetherby, Technical Assistant Ball speaking."

"Yes, Mr Ball?"

"My supervisor has asked me to phone you, sir." Hennessey thought Ball sounded young, his voice seemed to Hennessey to shake with fear and uncertainty. "The photograph you sent to us by courier of the Russian lady..."

"Yes...?"

"I am to tell you that it matches perfectly with the photograph of the skull taken at the pathology laboratory at the York District Hospital, title ref no, 30/08. I am further to tell you that a fax confirming the match will be dispatched post-haste...with respect, sir."

"I see...well, my compliments to your supervisor, thank him for the information."

"Yes, sir. Thank you, sir."

Hennessey replaced the receiver. He took hold of the file and wrote Svetlana Zvonoreva against the file number. He then picked up the phone again and jabbed the zero button. His call was answered rapidly.

"Switchboard." The voice was clipped, efficient.

"DCI Hennessey."

"Yes, sir."

"I want you to connect me with Interpol."

"Interpol? Well…I mean, yes, sir."

"Are you surprised?" Hennessey allowed his smile to be heard down the phone line.

"Frankly, yes, sir, I am. Never done it before."

"Well, there'll be a way, find it, whatever it is and connect me…soon as you like."

"Yes sir." The operator replaced the phone quickly, clearly anxious to address an interesting job. Hennessey knew that a senior officer's 'protocol' dictated that he should have the privilege of putting his phone down first, but felt disinclined to pursue the matter, it was in the scheme of things trifling to the extreme, and he didn't want to dampen the switchboard operator's enthusiasm.

Hennessey opened the file and added a brief note to the recording that a positive identification had been made. The 'ice maiden,' as he had come to refer to the corpse, though only privately, was now Svetlana Zvonoreva. He glanced at the clock on the wall. It was approaching midday, time for a stroll out, for a pub lunch, but he had done little that morning and wanted the sense of satisfaction of having completed something or set something in motion to enable him to enjoy his lunch, and so he waited until the switchboard operator called him back. He waited for ten minutes, during which he added recording to cases which had not been written up for a few days and read memos and circulars. For some reason, in response to some trigger he couldn't identify, his thoughts wandered to his childhood home in Greenwich, to the walk by the Thames, to the graceful Cutty Sark, so elegant on the outside, so disappointingly cramped within the hull. Then the phone brought his mind sharply back to the here and now. He picked it up after the third ring and calmly said, "DCI Hennessey."

"Switchboard, sir."

"Yes?"

"It's all in jargon, sir"

"What is?"

"The way to contact Interpol. The gentleman I spoke to said all UK police forces interface with Interpol via the portal at New Scotland Yard, London…interface…portal…that's what he said."

Hennessey groaned. He cared not for newspeak, and was gratified to realise that the switchboard operator who was, by the sound of his voice, still nearer his beginning than his end, should also express a dislike for trendy English. "I assume that means you have to phone New Scotland Yard and ask for 'Interpol', sir."

"I assume it does. Can I have an outside line, please?"

"Certainly, sir."

The line clicked and Hennessey heard the warm hum of the 'outside line-acquired' tone in his ear. He consulted his personal telephone book, dialled New Scotland Yard and asked to be put through to Interpol. Without a word in response being said, the line clicked again and a serious and officious sounding female voice said, "Interpol." Hennessey identified himself and related the edited story of the discovery of the remains of Svetlana Zvonoreva, late of St. Petersburg, the confirmation of her identity and her passport number as recorded in the missing person's report. He asked that her parents be informed.

"Will do…fax the police in St. Petersburg immediately, sir. Do you seek any information?"

Hennessey paused. "Confess that didn't occur to me, but if she mentioned in any letter the name of a friend and places she was visiting...any information really."

"Leave it to me, sir."

"Thank you." He replaced his phone, and did so first on this occasion. Something was moving, things were in hand. Time, he thought, for lunch.

Having lunched once again in the Starre Inne, and once again having seen the harshly singing busker and the sweet-playing violin players, and being pleased to note that the waiflike girl with the puppy was nowhere to be seen, he returned to Micklegate Bar Police Station. On the return journey he walked the pavement, for a change, and regretted his decision as the car and bus fumes reached him and caused him to feel nauseous. He wondered how long a fax would take to reach St. Petersburg. He wondered how efficient the police in St. Petersburg were. Nineteen when she died, Svetlana Zvonoreva would doubtless have some living relations, and most probably both parents would still be alive, as would any sibling. Soon a family would be weeping, if they were not already distraught, but at least they would know what had happened to their beautiful daughter/sister/cousin, who had left so excitedly for her year of study in England, only to disappear within three months of arriving there. But now the grieving and the closure can begin. Hennessey wanted to make a good show of this one, not simply in the interests of Anglo-Russian relations, but more on a human, personal level. He wanted to do what he could for a family in another country, a family whom he would never meet, whose daughter had ventured in all correctness into his patch, and who had lost her life – on his patch. He wanted to do well for them, for the family Zvonoreva, of St Petersburg.

Hennessey entered the welcoming shade of the police station and signed in. He walked down the CID corridor and glanced into Somerled Yellich's office as he passed.

Yellich was at his desk, just sitting there, patting his stomach.

"Productive morning, Yellich?" Hennessey stood in the doorframe.

"Oh..." Yellich turned to his senior officer and smiled. "Yes, boss. Just had lunch in the canteen...stodge...too heavy for this weather, should have had a salad. But yes, some leads."

Hennessey entered Yellich's office and sat down without being invited to do so, in the chair in front of Yellich's desk. "So, tell me."

Yellich told him of the visit to the university, to Jayne Style and the three artefacts recovered from the plastic bag containing Svetlana Zvonoreva's possessions.

"The bag is still there?"

"Yes, boss. The good citizen Style had me replace it for her, in the crawl space beneath her living room. Sara's going to have a fit when she sees my jacket and trousers, they'll need to be taken to the dry cleaners."

Hennessey smiled. "So, anything in the address book?"

"Plenty, but I don't think there's anything for us, skipper."

Yellich handed the address book to Hennessey. "It's all in that weird Russian writing, any English contact would surely have been entered in English?"

"Cyrillic."

"Sorry, boss?" Yellich, dark haired, balanced features, turned to Hennessey.

"Cyrillic. That weird 'Russian writing' as you call it is properly referred to as Cyrillic."

"Ah..." Yellich shrugged. "Okay. Anyway, it's all in that...Cyrillic stuff. I presume it's the address of her family and mates in Russia."

"Who have been notified of her death."

"The positive ID came in?"

"While you were out. I had to interface with the Interpol portal to transmit sad tidings."

"Sorry...?"

"Never mind. So there's a book of matches, someone called Leo and an outfit called Liaisons with an address here in the 'famous and fair?'"

"Yes, boss."

"Work for this afternoon, methinks."

"Methinks too, sire."

"Well I'll do one for you...they're not two handers."

"Doesn't seem like it, boss." Yellich held eye contact with Hennessey. "So, senior officer privilege."

"I'll go with the book of matches, let you explore the Liaisons connection."

"Very good, boss."

The girl walked to the man's house. An observer would see a short, slender, pale, waiflike figure, a small black dog on a length of string trotting obediently beside her. She wore only a thin cheesecloth shirt, faded denims and torn sports shoes. She went to the back of the house and knocked on the door. The man answered it, responding speedily to the soft yet desperate sounding knocking. Moments later the waif child was eating a substantial meal and her dog similarly was eating quality dog food with a substantial bowl of fresh water to slake its thirst afterwards.

"They found the body," she said.

"I know. It's been on the news," the man sat and watched her eat, "found it more quickly than I thought."

"Some guy stumbled across her. I was watching him crashing through the wood. He doesn't know nature, had no sensitivity for the green wood."

"Did the police find your hide?"

"No, the thickness of the wood was too much for them. I am sorry, Leo, I thought it would be a good place to leave the body."

The man smiled a kindly smile. "Don't blame yourself, it was a good place...as soon as I saw it, I knew it was a good place, just bad luck that birdwatcher came along, just bad luck that he chose the path he chose."

"Wasn't a path." The girl forked the beef stew hungrily.

"The route then, you know what I mean."

"Yes."

"How long will you stay in the wood? I do worry about you."

"All summer. My hide is dry...a little rain got in the other day but nothing compared with what fell outside, the lake is clean, I wash my clothes in it... I like being a wood nymph." She smiled and again he saw a warmth in her.

"Any more junk?"

"Not for a while, look." She pulled up her sleeve and showed a forearm heavy with fading track marks. "That's the last one and that was two weeks ago."

"Good. I am pleased." The man was short, silver hair cut short, a silver moustache, even seeing him for the first time the same observer who observed the waif girl would see that he was a shadow of his earlier self. "That does you no good, that stuff."

"I know. That's why I am living in the hide, the craving is less if I know it's not there to be had. If I was back in the squat, I would be puncturing myself...I just know I would."

"Still begging?"

The waif girl nodded. Most folk ignore me. Yesterday though, an old copper bought me some sandwiches. He was a nice old man, reminded me of you, but I think he was more concerned about Larry." She nodded at her small black mongrel. "Bought some water for him to drink and told me to take him out of the sun…black and brown dogs don't take well to the heat."

"No dogs do, but that man was right, dark dogs suffer badly in the sun."

"He threatened to arrest me, have Larry put into kennels. That would destroy me, it's only Larry that keeps me going."

"You would have got him back."

"Would I?" The girl finished her stew and placed the knife and fork centrally.

"Oh yes, not enough there to amount to cruelty. And you'd only be in the cells for the night."

"Really?" The girl looked hopefully at the man. "I thought they could take dogs off you…permanently."

"They can under some circumstances. It would take more than begging and a night in the cells to separate you from Larry."

The girl sighed with relief. "I don't want to take him into the city again, though, didn't realise I was making him suffer."

"You can leave him here, he'll be alright with me, pick him up when you come here with your pockets bulging with cash."

"A few quid if I am lucky." She forced a smile.

"You'll need somewhere else to live…the summers don't last."

"I've noticed. What are the winters like here?"

"Very cold. The east wind. Comes all the way from Siberia to chill your bones."

"Cornwall has mild winters. This will be my first winter north of London."

"Well take it from me, you'll need a good dry drum. And you'll need clothing. The trick is to dress from the inside out – thermals, under everything."

"Thermal underwear, that's for grannies."

"Not in the Vale in winter." The man stood and picked up the waif-girl's plate. Fancy some ice cream?"

"Oh…yes…"

"Well you needed the beef stew for your strength, even on a day like this, but you can have ice cream for pudding. My treat."

"Why do you do this?"

"This?"

"Give me food?"

"Because you are not eating."

"But you don't want anything in return."

"Why should I want anything in return?" He carried the plate to the sink and placed it in a bowl of soapy water.

"Because everybody else does. You can survive by selling your body, boys as well as girls…but it's easier for girls…but you don't seem to want that."

"Well…" he crossed the floor of the kitchen, cool with its north facing window and tiled floor, to a large refrigerator, he opened the fridge and took a packet of ice cream, which he carried back to the table, "I wouldn't want 'it' like that anyway, but now I don't want it at all. You see, Emily, you will find this…" he sliced off a generous portion of vanilla ice cream and laid it in a dish, which he placed in front of the girl. "You see age…and ageing, we don't grow old at the same rate. The years pass at the same speed but some retain youthfulness longer than others and, conversely, some people age more rapidly than others. I am in my mid sixties. I catch sight of myself in the mirror and think I have seen younger looking octogenarians."

"Octo…?"

"Folk in their eighties."

"Oh…"

"Anyway, the desire is no longer there. I have no energy for it anymore, for me desire and performance have both evaporated."

"You are taking more care of me than my own father ever did." She scraped the last of the ice cream from the bowl and once again placed the spoon centrally. "From the moment you bought me that meal..."

"You looked hungry."

"But you don't want anything, and I feel so safe with you...yet you asked me if I knew anywhere you could hide a body?"

The man looked at the city waif-girl, Emily, and said, simply, "Yes."

Chapter Three

Friday, 2nd August, 14.00 hours
in which Hennessey follows a trail through Olde Yorke, is later at home to the gracious reader, and Yellich hears a lovely story.

The shop was called Fashion and seemed to Hennessey to be a boutique, full of modern clothing in bright colours and various accessories, belts of intertwining leather, hats and inexpensive jewellery. The girl behind the glass topped counter seemed amused by Hennessey's presence, probably, he thought, because she was unused to old, grey tweedies making purchases in Fashion.

"Can I help you?" The girl smiled in a patronising manner.

"Police." Hennessey showed his ID and the smile vanished. "I'd like to talk to the manager."

The girl slid sideways from behind the counter and glided across the floor to a door upon which she knocked twice. Hennessey heard a male voice saying "Yes!" in an impatient tone. The girl opened the door, went into the room, and closed the door behind her. She reappeared moments later and said, "If you'll follow me, please." She walked back to the door, opened it and said. "The police, Mr Tamm."

"Thank you, Juliette." Tamm was a youthful looking man with what Hennessey thought was the hard expression and cold eyes of an experienced businessman who had seen troubled times. An old head on young shoulders: ought, he thought, to go far in the clothing retail industry. His office was like the occupant, cold and hard to Hennessey's view. No decoration at all, files, and filing cabinets, a desk covered in paper. "Yes?" Tamm eyed Hennessey with suspicion.

"What is it now?" There was fear in his voice.

"Know you, do we?" Hennessey allowed a softness to enter his voice. Heavens, he thought, the place definitely needed softening. Someone had to do it.

"This and that. But once you get known, you're known and the boys in blue never leave you alone. So what's it about?"

"What do you think?"

Tamm made to speak, then checked himself. "Haven't a clue." He leaned back in his chair. "Why don't you tell me?" He folded his arms in a defensive posture.

"Liaisons."

"What?" He was nervous.

"Liaisons." Hennessey felt the apparent 'hardness' evaporating.

"What's that?"

"Now it's me that hasn't a clue. I was hoping you could tell me. About three years ago, an outfit by that name occupied these premises."

Tamm relaxed; Hennessey saw that he was visibly relieved. "Oh...did they? I wouldn't know, I've been here for less than a year. Keeping my head above water, but that's about all."

Hennessey looked beyond Tamm, out of the windows behind him to the yard, which clearly belonged to the shop unit occupied by Fashion and to the gleaming black Porsche 911. Tamm was evidently keeping his head above water with some considerable style but he refrained from comment. "So you know nothing about Liaisons?"

"Not a thing."

"So, who would tell me?"

"Malton and Pickering Retail Lets."

"Where are they?"

"In the *Yellow Pages*."

"And your first name is?" Hennessey reached for his notebook and ballpoint.

"Why do you want to know?"

"For the sake of completion."

"I have nothing to do with Liaisons or whatever it's called."

"Just…tell…me… your…name…please."

Tamm paused.

"The first one, the one your mother uses."

"Used. She's deceased."

"Sorry to hear that."

"I'm not."

"So, the name?"

"Walter."

"Okay, Walter." Hennessey wrote in his pad. "And your date of birth?"

"Over 21."

"Alright Mr Tamm, thank you, you've been very helpful."

"My pleasure," said with clear sarcasm.

"So who occupied this unit before you did?"

"Don't know – it was empty. I took the rental."

"I see…very well, thanks." Hennessey turned and walked out of Tamm's cramped office, across the shop floor, feeling the eyes of the shop assistant on him as he did so. He opened the door and stepped out into narrow Long Close Lane. The sun beat down, beads of sweat ran from his scalp down his forehead and the nape of his neck. He plunged his hand into his pocket and took out his mobile phone and keyed in the stored number for Micklegate Bar Police Station."

"Police, Micklegate Bar. Constable Barnes speaking."

"DCI Hennessey, Barnes."

"Yes, sir."

Hennessey stopped walking and made use of the small shade offered by a doorway of an empty shop unit which had become a receptacle for pizza wrappers and soft drink cartons. "Do you have a copy of the *Yellow Pages* to hand?"

"Yes, sir."

"Okay. Look up Malton and Pickering Retail Lets."

"Malton and Pickering Retail Lets?"

"That's it...and while you're doing that put me through to CR please."

"Very good, sir."

The line clicked. Hennessey heard the ringing tone. Then a female voice said, "Criminal Records."

"DCI Hennessey."

"Yes, sir."

"I want anything you've got on one Walter Tamm. Looks to be in his late twenties but I can't give precise numbers. Business address is Fashion, it's a trendy clothes shop at the corner of Long Close Lane, number 132."

"Got that, sir. Are you in the building?"

"No, place what you've got in my pigeonhole, please."

"Yes, sir."

"Good...appreciated. Put me back to switchboard, please."

Once again the line clicked and once again Hennessey heard the ringing tone, which ended when DC Barnes said, "DC Barnes speaking."

"Hennessey."

"Yes, sir. I have found an entry for Malton and Pickering Retail Lets...do you want the number?"

"No. The address, please."

"Very good, sir, it is in Lady Pecketts Yard."

"Where's that?"

"It's a snickelway, sir."

"Yes...?"

"It's in the corner of Fossgate and Pavement."

"Do you have a street map there?"

"Yes, sir."

"I am on Long Close Lane...which is the best route to take?"

Barnes paused. "Turn right into George Street, sir."

"Yes..."

"Left on Walmgate...stay on Walmgate until it becomes Fossgate."

"Got it."

"Look for Cheats Lane on your left just before you get to the junction with Pavement. That's also a snickelway..."

"I see."

"Cheats Lane will take you into Lady Pecketts Yard."

"Any number for Malton and Pickering's?"

"No, sir, just the name Lady Pecketts Yard."

"Alright. Thank you." Hennessey switched off the mobile. He set off to walk as speedily as comfort in that heat would allow, in accordance to the directions given by Constable Barnes, and pondered whether technology was progressing, or was it driving humankind to its own destruction? He was not sorry to be approaching retirement, and was quite content to hand the world to its youth.

Hennessey left Fashion, nestling as it did next to the Phoenix pub and turned right on George Street. Acting on a whim, he thought he would visit the grave of John Palmer, otherwise known as Dick Turpin, whose ride from London on Black Bess has become the stuff of legend. Hennessey once read of Turpin's execution on the gallows situated on the site of what is now York racecourse, specifically between what is now the stand and the first bend where the ground forms a slope. People in their hundreds had sat in tiers on the slope and watched as Turpin climbed the ladder to the platform; his leg had faltered and seemed to collapse;

he stamped the leg to steady himself, and once upon the platform, the noose round his neck, he chatted to the executioner and called out to the crowd for fully thirty minutes, before flinging himself head first in what was a successful attempt to snap his neck and thus avoid a slow death by strangulation. It was clearly the way of it in 1739, wherein executions were not only public, but the condemned was expected to entertain the crowd, who had, after all, in many cases, come a long way to see him. Dick Turpin's grave had, observed Hennessey, clearly been reconstituted at some point between 1739 and the present day, being the only legible, and the only vertical stone in the small cemetery. He turned from the grave and resumed his walk, following the curve of George Street until it met narrow Walmgate directly opposite the offices of the *York Evening Press*, where he turned left. He crossed over the cobbled humpbacked bridge that spanned the still, canalised waters of the River Foss by the Hospital, a school building dated 1812, 'the foundation stone was laid in the 53rd year of the reign of King George III,' and now clearly used as flats. In front of him the skyline was interrupted, and dominated by the tower of the Minster. He walked past Cheats Lane – being a snickelway it was easy to miss – and realising what he had done when he reached bustling Pavement, retraced his steps. Cheats Lane, he found, was open to the sky and even boasted space for a car or two to be parked. He followed it to the right and entered Lady Pecketts Yard, a small, but very proper snickelway, narrow, with steps along its length and partially covered. An old lamp attached to the wall opposite a Tudor fronted building was, he thought, very York; the short snickelway pleased him, and within it he located the premises of Malton and Pickering Retail Lets'.

* * *

"He just couldn't make it pay," John Redfern shrugged. "You get to know the business community in this line of work."

"And you got to know Luke Brogan?"

"Yes." John Redfern sat back on his chair. His office was small, low beams, plaster walls, very old York, in Hennessey's view. The only chair that Redfern could offer was a wooden upright dining chair but Hennessey was grateful to accept it. The walk from Long Close Lane he had found tiring, not because of the distance but more because of the relentless beating of the sun combined with the pavements and walls which also radiated heat. It had been pleasant to enter the cool of Cheat's Lane and from there the cool of Lady Peckett's Yard, and still more pleasant to enter the even cooler premises of the Malton and Pickering Retail Lettings. "Brogan..." he shrugged. "What can I say? A bit of a wide boy...a man full of business ideas and no business sense. I have let to him on a few occasions..."

"You got your money, though?"

"Oh yes, rent in advance. We own over one hundred shop units in the Vale, from York to Scarborough. Some, many in fact, remain viable over a long period of time, others...well, you know the ones that won't make it, inappropriate for the area...we offer advice but it's not always heeded. Folk who open a shop selling domestic goods, like soap and brushes and dishcloths and other such inexpensive knick-knacks, in a student area where only fast food and alcohol outlets survive, is but one example." Redfern wore a jacket and tie, he had close cropped hair and a pencil moustache. "Folk like that lose money, buy in goods wholesale, pay an expensive commercial rent and take little or nothing into the till. Seen them pack up...always the same...grim faced, a look of being cheated as they carry their unsold goods from the shop unit into the back of a van…and very often it's a husband and wife team…start out with such high hopes, then worry sets in, then fear, then acceptance and they phone us and regret they can't meet the rent, which is due. Some even say 'We should have listened to you'."

"Did you advise Luke Brogan?"

"Yes…and he didn't listen and he didn't survive."

"So, what about Liaisons?"

"A dating agency, as the name implies. I know little of how it worked, but I think they interviewed clients on video, then matched them with other clients who could view the videos…not an original idea, but his problem was that he was under funded and had a bad location. You have visited Long Close Lane?"

"Yes."

"It's about as far out of the way as you could get and yet remain within the walls. He needed a more central location and bigger and better advertising…spent money on promotional gimmicks, like pens and lighters."

"Yes, we have one and the trail led here."

"Really?" Redfern nodded. "He gave me one, too…used it as well…never look a gift horse in the mouth, but he should have spent money on advertising. Instead he contented himself with a few handmade posters which he put up in various places…not quite fly posting…but in shop windows, places like that."

"I see."

"He gave them out quite liberally, many people received them."

Hennessey felt a pang of disappointment. He felt the inquiry to be in danger of losing momentum. "Where is Luke Brogan now, do you know?"

"I'm afraid I don't, though doubtless he'll be involved

with some get-rich-quick scheme."

"You sound as though you don't like him, Mr Redfern?"

"I don't. Just couldn't take to the fellow and it doesn't surprise me that the police are taking an interest in him."

"We are not." Hennessey leaned forward and rested his elbows on his knees clasping his hands together. "We are following a trail, a link with the frozen corpse...you will have read about it."

"Oh yes...how strange."

"Well, leads are thin on the ground, and one lead is the Liaisons lighter which was among her possessions, kept by her former landlady, good woman, but it seems it means little."

"That's for the police to decide, all I can say is that Brogan distributed those pens and cigarette lighters willy-nilly, so it may be relevant...it may not."

"Feels like a cul-de-sac." Hennessey stood. "Well, thanks for your time Mr Redfern. He turned to the door of Redfern's office. "Strange, Fashions is thriving...some way out of the way location."

"It's a specialist shop, a trendy boutique, specialist shops don't necessarily need to be well placed. Tamm took that shop over from Brogan."

"Really?" Hennessey turned back to face Redfern. "Tamm gave me the impression it was vacant for some time before he moved in, not in so many words, just the impression I received."

"It's the wrong impression. It was vacant, it had to be, but Brogan moved out the day before Tamm moved in. In fact Tamm came to see me about the let before Brogan moved out."

"He did?"

"Yes. Brogan told him he was having to give up the let."

"Wait a minute...Tamm and Brogan know each other?"

"Yes."

"That's interesting because Tamm told me he didn't know Brogan…and that was said in so many words."

"Well, I can assure you, Mr Hennessey, they do know each other. I do not know the nature of the relationship but they do know each other, possibly on first name terms, too. I remember it like yesterday, Tamm phoned me and said that he understood that Luke Brogan was giving up the let on Long Close Lane. I remember it because that's the first inkling I had that Liaisons was in trouble."

"I see," Hennessey held eye contact with Redfern, "I see," he said again. "Now that is interesting, probably not relevant to this inquiry but interesting nonetheless. What do you know of Tamm?"

"Not the sort of man I'd want my daughter to bring home. He's a harder case than Brogan. I can see Brogan falling under his spell; I can see Tamm leading Brogan astray. I found that there was something about Brogan that made him easily led."

"Again, interesting. Well, thank you, Mr Redfern, thank you indeed."

Outside once again, on sun drenched pavements under a vast blue sky, Hennessey tramped to the Duck and Drake nightclub, which stood on The Stonebow near the entrance to Black Horse Pass, and was thus a mercifully short walk for the good officer. He rang the doorbell and a silver squawk box set in the wall beside the door said, "Yes?" Hennessey closed to it and said "Police." Instantly the door clicked open and the squawk box said, "Pull the door shut behind you, please." Hennessey stepped into the nightclub and obligingly shut the door behind him. The lights inside the club were turned up and he saw clearly the darkened walls and maroon seating area and could easily imagine the ambience created by dimmer lighting and a youthful clientele. A man behind the bar polished glasses and looked at him once and then seemed to forget him. A middle-aged lady pushing and pulling a vacuum cleaner across a carpeted area didn't even spare him a glance. A woman, dressed in a smart grey business suit approached him, "Police?" she asked.

"Yes," Hennessey smiled and nodded. He thought her to be in her early thirties. She was blonde, had highlights in her hair, loud scarlet polish on her nails to match her high-heeled shoes and she wore rings and bracelets, and chains around her neck.

"This way, please, sir." She turned and walked erect, soldier-like, almost marching, deeper into the building. Hennessey followed and was led to a doorway that was well camouflaged within the wall, painted black with a small black handle. The woman knocked on it, twice.

"Yes?" The voice, male, called from within.

The woman opened the door and stepped into the room. "The police, Mr Conner."

"Thanks, Wendy." Connor stood and Wendy withdrew, leaving the two men to talk. Connor smiled, "Come in, please, Mr..."

"Hennessey."

"It's good of you to come, we don't like this in our club. Please take a seat."

"Oh?" Hennessey sat as invited.

"Yes, what my young lady calls the 'flip side' of York...sometimes the 'darker side', but she's right."

Connors sat heavily. Hennessey saw him to be overweight, badly out of condition...heavy of the jowls and by his thick lensed spectacles, equally heavily deficient in eyesight. He grabbed a cigarette from a packet with meaty paws. "Smoke?"

"Not for me, thanks."

"I shouldn't, the doctor says I am killing myself but if I didn't have a nerve calmer once every few minutes...well, I couldn't carry on. Never go into the nightclub business, Mr Hennessey."

"Actually, I have no plans to do so, I have other plans for my retirement and they don't include the glitz and the glamour of dancing the night away and dropping ecstasy tablets. I intend to take up landscape painting if truth be told. Ideal for a retired man with an active dog."

"Sounds like heaven...but the fight last night, it's that darker side of York, the tourists don't see it, walking the walls, crowding into the Minster, sending their children for rides on the 'steamie' at the railway museum. 'What a pretty little city' they say. They don't see the farm workers come in for their beer of a night or the coal miners from Selby pit, and that's what happened last night. Two groups...made the club look like a saloon in Dodge City, except stools don't splinter spectacularly when they get put over someone's head. Photography."

"Sorry?"

"I should have been a photographer, sitting for hours outside the house of a famous person waiting for said celeb to appear and if they didn't appear it wouldn't be my fault so I wouldn't lose my job with the newspaper. That's a job for me, getting paid to do nothing all day. So what can I do?"

"Well, mid-life career changes are not unknown, though I couldn't advise you on how to enter photojournalism."

Conner pulled strongly on the nail and wafted the smoke away as he exhaled. "No...no...my security, the cops who came to unravel the bodies last night, said they would send someone to advise my how to tighten up my security on the door and also inside. That's what you're here for, isn't it?"

"No, actually I am not."

"Oh...?" Conner looked surprised, then disappointed, then alarmed. It was the alarmed look that interested Hennessey. Conner was a man with a secret he wished to be kept well away from the police. Hennessey had seen that look many, many times. "Well what can I do for you?"

Hennessey took the book of matches from his pocket and handed them to Conner. Conner picked them up, and examined them. He opened them and read 'Leo'. "Well, if you're going to ask me who Leo is, I am afraid I don't know."

"Well, I was...if only because long shots have paid off before. It may have been that Leo was a known name, someone strongly associated with the club, for example."

"Well, he wasn't...you are right, Mr...sorry...?"

"Hennessey."

"Sorry, I'm dreadful for names. People do get associated with businesses but no one by the name Leo has ever been associated with the Duck and Drake. I opened the club...used to be a bank, a branch of the Yorkshire Penny Bank, so called."

"That's going back a long time. I remember the Yorkshire Penny Bank," Hennessey sat back in his chair, "always thought it very quaint."

"You don't sound like a Yorkshireman?"

"London, Greenwich."

"Ah...well, they dropped the 'penny'...'the penny dropped'." Conner smiled at his own unintentional humour, "the penny dropped...thought it gave an old-fashioned and too provincial image, I dare say. Now it's the Yorkshire Bank plc and part of a large group owned by an Australian company."

"My, hasn't it grown?"

"It's called globalisation. Preferred the old, small independent banks myself, more down to the human scale…but I'm very sorry your journey has been wasted."

"Well, had to inquire for the sake of completeness. Can you tell me anything about the book of matches?"

"Old style. Use a different logo now. Stopped using these two years ago."

"Did you give them to anyone special?"

"No, they were complimentary, bowls of them on the bar and on the tables. Any customer could have picked one up."

"I see. What about this young lady?" Hennessey handed Conner the photograph of Svetlana Zvonoreva, a copy of which had been retained in the missing persons file.

"Well," Conner smiled, "a nightclub is not like a pub, Mr Hennessey, we don't get to know our clients unless they cause trouble – like the crew last night – then they get scratched and we never see them again. She's a very attractive young woman, wouldn't be short of male attention in this or any other club."

"But you don't recognise her?"

"I don't." Conner tapped the photograph. "Jamie might, depends on how old this photograph is."

"Three years."

"Well, Jamie has been with me for four years. He's utterly humourless, no sense of humour at all, but a damn good barman and an astounding memory for faces. He might even know who Leo is or was. I'll introduce you. He's at the bar now, getting ready."

"Thanks," Hennessey stood, "but no thanks. I saw him when I came in, I can introduce myself. What about that young woman, Sally was it? How long has she been with you?"

"With me about five years, that's my young lady that I mentioned, the one who refers to the 'flip side' of York…or the 'dark side', but she's only been employed in the club for the last six months."

Jamie was, Hennessey saw, a lean young man, lean in figure and lean in face. He was dark haired, and, Hennessey thought, his eyes small and piercing and as Conner had said, seemingly devoid of humour. He looked at the photograph of Svetlana Zvonoreva, then he said, "The Russian girl."

Hennessey's heart jumped. "Yes."

"Haven't seen her for a long time…two years, possibly more…"

"You can't have."

"I just assumed she'd gone back to Russia but I later found out she had gone missing."

"Yes…"

"Has she turned up?"

"Yes."

"No longer with us?" Jamie paused, "Well, you would not be here otherwise."

"Well, she could be alive and well having been held against her will these last three years."

"True…three years…didn't know it was as long as that, I thought two, time passes quickly."

"For the lucky ones."

"Aye… Her name is, or was, Svetlana."

"Was…your assumption was correct. And yes, we know her name. Anything else you recall?"

Jamie wiped a standard white tea cloth inside of a half-pint glass. He wore a red shirt, black trousers. A watch, inexpensive, was his only decoration. "Well, she came in with a group…this was as you say a few years ago, every Friday night during term time. An odd bunch, Americans, Russians, Italians…every nationality under the sun. Turns out it was the Foreign Students Society."

"The Foreign Students Society?"

"Yes, at the university…one of the societies organised by the students; swimming club, hiking club…beer drinking society."

"They have a beer drinking society?" Hennessey was genuinely amused.

"Yes, I was in it. I was at York, took a degree in philosophy which I can't do anything with. I want to make a life for myself in the licensed retail trade, want to be a publican. Running a bar and a nightclub seemed like good training. I started as bar staff, now I manage it, move to a public house soon, get known by the personnel section of a Brewery. But I was in the beer drinking society…we took ourselves very seriously. It was much more than sitting about quaffing amber nectar, we promoted real ale. We organised the annual real-ale convention in York. We did what we could to promote new breweries and support struggling ones if we thought their beer worth saving."

"I see."

"We took trips out to ailing pubs to do what we could to save them, put our money their way, especially if it was believed such a pub was going to be renovated and turned into a 'plastic theme pub'."

"I confess you and I are on the same wavelength there, Mr…?"

"Donovan. James Donovan."

"Mr Donovan."

"Svetlana's friends were the Foreign Students Society. It's quite lonely being a foreign student and so a few years ago, about ten, I think, a French student and a Danish student both doing their one-year study of English decided to form the Foreign Students Society. It's not original, many universities have such a society…get approval from the Student Union…get a bit of a grant. Only requirement for entry is that you have to be foreign… bit of a lonely hearts club really, just provided a meeting point for isolated people in a strange country...helped their conversational English too, all communication was in English, which is what they had in common."

"So she may be remembered? I mean, by the present students in that Society?"

"Maybe, but my understanding is that the vast majority were in the UK for one year only as part of a degree course in their home nation."

"Ah..."

"But not all, one or two were PhD students at York for the full three stretch. Might be worth paying them a call."

"Might well be. Do you recall any of her friends?"

"Strange...I can see the group now, they favoured that table at the edge of the seating area, but their faces are a blur. I can't see Svetlana in my mind's eye but I recognise the photo of her."

"I see. Name Leo mean anything?"

"Not a thing. Leo...a nickname, short for Leonard...a real name in itself."

"Exactly. Could be anything...might not even be a man."

"Indeed. Well, I don't, not a Leo associated with Svetlana. Did know a woman who liked being called Leo because that was her star sign, but that was in another country and besides the wench is dead...literally."

"I see." Hennessey put the photograph back inside his jacket pocket. "Well, thanks...Foreign Student Society...it's a help, one more stone to turn over, the inquiry inches forward."

"So what did happen to her?"

"Well, that is what we want to find out."

Jamie Donovan betrayed a thin streak of humour as his lips curled in a self-deprecating smile. "Yes, point to you. I meant where was her body found? Must have been badly decomposed. How do you know it is her? DNA samples...?"

"It wasn't actually...decomposed, I mean." Hennessey enjoyed the look of surprise in Donovan's eyes, "and identity was done by photography. Read the newspaper, watch television news or listen to the radio?"

"I don't get much chance..." Donovan's voice tailed away.

"Well, pick up a copy of the *Post* tomorrow. We've asked for media assistance...should be quite a splash...probably front page stuff. Thanks anyway."

Hennessey walked out of the Duck and Drake into the heat of mid afternoon. Stonebow was not his favourite part of York, architecturally speaking, all 1960s slab sized brutalism. He strolled back through to the centre of the ancient town, making use of what shade he could find. He enjoyed the walk once out of The Stonebow. The Stonebow he found to be curved and angled and concrete with its medium size square office block, it was an area in the centre of the city which in Hennessey's mind was just 'not York'. It was an area which could be part of any new town development of the 1960s and the 1970s. He walked into Pavement, threading his way through the shoppers and the tourists and passing a paramedic cyclist in his distinctive yellow jacket chatting to another man. He took the right fork at All Saints Church and entered the hump-backed pedestrian precinct that was High Ousegate. Hennessey disliked pedestrian precincts, believing them to encourage unsavoury folk to cities in the night time and where such folk loiter there is often work for the police to deal with. A traffic flow on the other hand keeps a street alive, and prevents people being able to wander from one side of the road to the other. He walked down the further slope of High

Ousegate into Ousegate, heavy with traffic and over Ouse Bridge, observing the new development along both sides of the river, save for the older buildings of King's Staith, below and to his left. He walked across George Hudson Street, by the plaque set in the wall, dedicated to the 'Railway King' in whose honour the street was named, despite ample evidence that in life he had been a shady and corrupt individual, and entered the winding, gentle slope of Micklegate, with its shops, eateries, pubs and ancient buildings off to his left.

The girl and he saw each other at the same time. The girl halted momentarily and then realising she couldn't avoid Hennessey, she continued walking. She avoided eye contact but George Hennessey stepped out and said "We meet again."

"Yes." The girl stopped.

"You haven't got your dog with you." He was pleased she had stopped. Many cop hating/distrusting heroin addicts would have walked on, stopping only if arrested.

"No."

"He's safe?"

"Larry...yes," she smiled, "he's well looked after. You don't need to worry about Larry, nobody could take better care of Larry than the old guy watching him for me. I told him about you, about what you said about black and brown dogs and heat."

"Good."

"He said you were right."

"What is your surname?" Hennessey took out his notebook.

"Why, am I being arrested?"

"No...but I could."

"For begging?" She held her hand up against the sun, salute-like, shielding her eyes.

"If I thought it would benefit you."

"For my own good? Where've I heard that before?"

"So tell me."

"Speake with an *e*"

"Speake with an *e*," Hennessey wrote. "First name?"

"Emily."

"Date of birth?"

Emily Speake parroted her numbers, which put her age at eighteen. Hennessey sighed, he thought that Emily Speake could pass for twelve if kitted out with a blouse and pleated shirt and ankle socks and sandals. Again he thought her waiflike, wasted looking. "Address?"

"None. Nothing permanent." But she thought "a hide in the thick wood near to where you found the body and wouldn't you like to know who put it there? But I'm not shopping Leo, not to you, matey, not to anyone...not after what Leo did for me."

"You going begging?" Hennessey closed his notebook.

"It's all I can do."

"That's not true...there's training courses."

"Yeah..." Emily Speake turned and walked down Micklegate, towards the good begging grounds, where plenty was to be had.

"I studied medieval history, for two terms at York, part of my overall degree from Brown." Mary Wilson sat on a scatter cushion in her room in the university lodgings, part of an old house just off the campus. Her rooms were in the attic of the house and her ceilings were low and deeply angled. Yellich was overwhelmed by the visual stimulation in the room, posters of American cities covered the greater part of the wall and ceiling space, one wall was given over to postcards neatly arranged in rows and columns and blue-tacked to the wall. Framed photographs of family and a pet dog, and a tall-seeming man, occupied horizontal surfaces, with potted plants, money plants and spider plants in the main, though one plant pot contained an oak tree sapling. "Returned for my PhD, completing it now, it's been hard work." Mary Wilson was a slender freckly-faced woman with a soft voice and warm, trusting eyes. A woman who had not by then been damaged by life, still possessing a certain naïvety. For her, Yellich felt, bad things, like people disappearing, possibly murdered, are things that happen to other people, like Svetlana Zvonoreva. "But yes, I remember Svetlana, I remember her very well. We roomed together at Ms Style's."

"Yes...and got on with each other very well by all accounts."

"She told you that?"

"Yes. Told me how you chatted to each other for hours on end."

"Yes." Mary Wilson smiled as if recalling a warm memory.

Yellich sat in a chair, which he found very comfortable indeed. It looked inexpensive and with wooden arms seemed to be hard, but the seat of the chair was generous in respect of its proportions and supported his legs; the back was of the ideal angle for his spine. "Well...what can you remember of her disappearance?"

"That she didn't return to Ms Style's one night."

"Do you know where she was going?"

"I think to meet a guy"

"Do you know who?"

"I am afraid I don't. I think it was a first time meet. Svetlana, lovely girl, she and I got on well but we really had different agendas. She did a little work, she had to, she would have got into trouble at home if she failed her year at York. It's a pressure on many Eastern Bloc and developing world students that isn't appreciated by us fortunate westerners. Their government picks up the tab for the tuition fees and accommodation fees and gives them some survival money...and that's not small beer...western tuition fees and living expenses for one student for one year could keep a whole family alive for ten years in some countries in the world. So if a student from those countries is given that investment, and fails to return with the requisite bit of paper, well..." Mary Wilson shrugged. "It's like goodnight Vienna for them."

"That hadn't occurred to me."

"Consequences of failing vary from country to country but some countries will imprison failed students."

"Really?"

"Oh yes...the really tyrannical regimes would, they need their English speakers, their scientists and engineers and they don't like losing money...that's a lot of pressure on foreign students...depending on their nationality."

"And Svetlana feared failing?"

"Yes..." again Mary Wilson shrugged and moved to a cross-legged lotus position, and by doing so revealed to Yellich she enjoyed great suppleness of limb, he thought her probably an exponent of yoga. He detected a certain inner calm about her as in one practised in meditation, "but..."

"But?"

"Yes. How to put this? Dear, Svetlana, what did happen to you that night? Dear, dear Svetlana..."

"You want and don't want to say something ill of her?" Yellich probed. "If it helps you...it will help Svetlana if you tell us anything, everything..."

"Yes," Mary Wilson smiled, "that's the correct attitude. Thank you..." She paused. "Well, she wasn't the most dedicated student I have met, she did enough...just enough. I don't think she would have failed but from what I saw of her work and the comments it attracted, she might have got her fingertips beyond the pass mark threshold but that's all...sufficient to prevent her going back to St. Petersburg shamefaced and empty handed but only just."

"She struggled with the work?"

"No, that's not what I am saying, she didn't apply herself as fully as she might have done. She was an intelligent woman, very intelligent, I thought her more able than I in that department but what potential she had, she lost because she didn't work to her capacity. Like I said, she had a different agenda."

"Being...?"

"Well, she did apply herself to her socialising, she worked hard at that...you see she was desperate to remain in the West."

"Yes...I had that impression."

"So she joined the Foreign Students Society, wanting to meet a western man...a French guy, a West German, a Dane...an American would have been ideal...and she also joined a dating agency."

"Liaisons?"

"Yes, that was it...they put posters up in the uni and round the town. They got taken down when they went up in the university at least, no right to put them up, you see, town-based business, but as soon as they were taken down they reappeared, went straight back up again. Anyway, if Svetlana didn't throw herself into her studies, she threw herself into finding a westerner, success there meant she didn't have to succeed in her studies, it was a gamble she seemed, like, prepared to take."

"I see. And you don't know who she was meeting that evening?"

"Nope."

"Or where?"

"No, but she wasn't afraid of going to bars alone. Well, she wasn't reckless...some bars she wouldn't venture into, but the more Bohemian bars where women would be safer, the more upmarket bars, for the same reason."

"I see."

"Do you know if she met anyone special? If she had a settled relationship with anyone at all?"

"Hardly had time. She arrived in the UK in September, disappeared when? In the fall...or autumn as I guess I should say...but no, no one special, I am sure she would have told me. And Ms Style was very protective of her 'gels' as she used to refer to us...no men allowed in the rooms but men were invited to call to collect their 'gel' and Ms Style would chat to them and assess their suitability. And Svetlana was a 'gel' who didn't get called on and collected for a date."

"So you don't remember anyone called Leo?"

"Leo?" Mary Wilson shook her head. "I'm real sorry...but never heard that name mentioned. Leo...it's a name that has a certain ring to it, it's a name that I would have remembered." Mary Wilson paused again. Yellich waited, she was remembering something. "I heard the news about the body being found in the woods...that was Svetlana?"

"Yes."

"Naked?"

"Yes."

"No jewellery left on her body?"

"None."

"So she was kept alive all these years?"

"No...she...well, her body was kept deep frozen."

"Ugh!" Mary Wilson shuddered.

"Why did you ask about her jewellery?"

"Well...I saw her just before she went out that night, she

was wearing her locket."

"Her locket?"

Mary Wilson stood and walked serenely over to a cupboard and knelt before it, very ladylike thought Yellich, back perfectly perpendicular; a book balanced on her head would not have fallen as she walked, knelt, selected a wide yellow folder, stood and returned to the scatter cushions. "My album," she said, "or at least one of them. I keep them by dates rather than subject matter and this one contains images of Svetlana." She leafed through the album. "And here is the one I think may be of interest..." She turned the album round and handed it to Yellich.

"Yes, that's her." Yellich looked at the colour print of Svetlana Zvonoreva, a face of conventional beauty, high cheekbones, blue eyes, a warm demure smile, lemon hair, a low-cut yellow dress. "And is that the locket?"

"That's the locket. She was very proud of it, her grandmother gave it to her. Her grandmother had worn it as a young woman and had given it to her. It was a family heirloom; it dated back to well before the 1917 revolution. It was said, so she told me, that her grandmother wore it when she met the man who became her husband, and her great great grandmother also wore it on the day she met the man who became her husband and it was given to Svetlana to help her find her husband on condition that she bequeath it to her first born granddaughter when said granddaughter came of age."

"Lovely story."

"If it had had a better ending, because I am certain that Svetlana was wearing it when she went out that night, when she walked out of good Ms Style's house for the last time."

"Really?"

"Yes, really...it's gold. What grade, what carat, I don't know but I think very high...it's valuable."

"Seems like it."

"She wore cheap rings and a watch from the Communist and immediate post-Communist era but that locket came from the era of the Tsars, it had survived a revolution, the purges, and two world wars, and had brought good luck to its two previous owners. But the point is, that while her rings and watch would have been thrown away as valueless, only an idiot would throw that locket away."

"Or a clever man."

Mary Wilson looked at him with a puzzled expression.

"I mean a clever, ruthless person would throw the locket away along with all else that could connect him with the murder, no matter how valuable it is or was."

"Yes, I see, but call it woman's intuition if you like, that locket is still with us. Ponder its history, ponder what upheavals it has survived, it has an inextinguishable life force. It's out there."

"May I keep this photograph?"

"Please do. It's the only one of her that shows the locket but it's a good one of the locket. It contained a photograph of her grandmother as a young woman wearing it. The locket will lead you to Svetlana's killer."

"Thanks." Yellich stood. "Please don't be angry about the university giving out your address, I did explain that you were not in any trouble and it was a major inquiry."

"Not at all," Mary Wilson also stood, seeming to elevate herself effortlessly. "You were lucky to catch me in."

"May I ask you where you are going to plant the oak tree?"

Mary Wilson looked at the oak sapling with a warm smile. "Oliver...that's his name, Oliver the oak tree, he's been with me three years now. I picked up the acorn from the street, there's a small oak tree near here, sheds its acorns on the sidewalk so I picked one up...rescued it from the squirrels...potted it...got a shoot in the spring. He has been with me throughout my PhD and now I am approaching the end of it I shall have to find Oliver a permanent home, somewhere prominent where he's got a good view...and hopefully I'll be able to return from time to time, once every few years to see how he's getting on," she stroked the leaves gently, "and who knows, in the fullness of time, I can introduce my children to him and then they their children."

It was, Yellich thought, a handsome attitude. He resolved then to do the same, and would pick up an acorn in the early autumn, though in his case, he was unlikely to be able to introduce the tree to his grandchildren. Again he felt a pang of sadness.

Hennessey sat at his desk and swilled the last of his tea around the bottom of his mug whilst looking at the photograph of Svetlana Zvonoreva. "The locket is shown quite clearly, it also looks to the untrained eye to be quite distinct. We need to photograph this photograph...specifically photograph the locket, have it magnified and issued to the press. I doubt the killer has kept it, he or she would indeed be foolish to do that."

"Indeed, boss." Yellich sat in the chair in front of Hennessey's desk.

"But he or she may have been tempted by its value and may have sold it to a jeweller, it's a line of inquiry that will be worth following." He handed the photograph back to Yellich. "Can you see to that?"

"Yes, boss, send it to Wetherby before I go home, ask the lab boys to do what they can, I'm sure they'll come up with the goods." He also drank cooling tea.

"Any future in chasing her friends in the Foreign Students Society?"

"Very little, I think, sir. Most of them were only there for a year, even those among the full three year degree will have gone home now."

"Alright." Hennessey paused. "Didn't take to the fellow Tamm of Fashions, denied knowing Brogan who ran Liaisons."

"Tamm of Fashions?" Yellich responded to the name.

"Yes, do you know him?"

"Yes, indeed I do, he's one of my slow moving cases."

"Well, wheels within wheels..."

"Clothing shop on Long Close Lane?"

"Yes."

"He is suspected of moving imitation clothing, fake designer gear."

"Really...now that is interesting, little wonder he was hostile towards the police. He also denied knowing Brogan who ran the Liaisons operation, and which it seems likely that Svetlana used, to hunt for Mr Westernman. If he still had his records, that would be most useful."

"What are you thinking, skipper? An introduction organised by the Liaisons turned out to be a murderously bad liaison?"

"Possibly...possibly a closer involvement. What track has Tamm got?"

"Very little, we have his prints on file because of some juvenile stuff, nothing since then but he's always where the bad news is, as though he gets others to do his dirty work."

"Yes, Mr Redfern at the letting agency said he was a 'hard case', and he could see Luke Brogan falling under his spell."

"We should visit Brogan and Tamm, methinks." Yellich stood and took Hennessey's empty mug. "Tamm will lead us to Brogan."

"Yes..." Hennessey mused, "it's the only lead we've got

and it's hardly a lead at all...that and the locket. But you know, I might just contact the Foreign Students Society, a few of them may recall her, yes...for the sake of completeness." He glanced at his watch. It was five-thirty p.m. "Won't be anybody there now, a student society, that will have to wait until Monday but we'll pay a call on Tamm tomorrow."

"Very good, boss." Yellich took the used mugs to the washroom to rinse them clean.

Hennessey drove home. The traffic was heavy upon leaving York and he was grateful for the company of soothing Radio Four. Upon approaching Easingwold, the traffic had thinned and he was able to turn into the drive of his detached house on the Thirsk Road without causing any interruption in the flow. He got out of his car and heard Oscar barking excitedly from within the house. He opened the front door and the mongrel ran at him with wagging tail, jumping up at him in joy at Hennessey's return, and Hennessey in turn knelt and patted his dog and toyed with his ears. Moments later, a mug of tea in hand, Hennessey stood on the patio at the rear of his house and spoke aloud. He was alone save for his dog, who, uncomfortable with the heat, had retreated to the shade of the kitchen. "Strange couple of days to end the week with," he said. "Corpse, three years old but frozen and perfectly preserved, but I told you that yesterday. Today, well, some leads but nothing you could call progress, not in a concrete sense anyway. Yellich and I will be picking them up tomorrow...two handing I suspect, we were single handing today. I'll let you know how it goes, but you know I will anyway. Things with my lady friend are comfortably settled, we exist on each other's horizon, not central to each other's lives and we both like it like that. We haven't the space for remarriage, neither of us. I know you are happy for us." The garden he spoke to had a lawn extending from the back of the house to a privet hedge which ran lengthways across the garden with a wrought iron gateway set half way along it. Beyond the hedge were two garden sheds which stood side by side to the left as viewed from the house, area beyond the hedge was given over to an orchard of eating and cooking apple trees. Beyond the orchard was a waste area, which George Hennessey's wife had called the 'going forth', having come across the phrase in Francis Bacon's essay 'Of Gardens'. The 'going forth' was left as nature intended, save for a pond which had been dug and where frogs had been introduced.

George and Jennifer Hennessey had moved into the house when newly married and he a junior constable. The rear garden had been a flat uninteresting slab of lawn, when heavily pregnant Jennifer Hennessey had sat down at the kitchen table and designed the rear garden. Four months later she was dead. Having given a proud George Hennessey a son, healthy and perfectly formed, she had, three months later, been walking in Easingwold when she collapsed. The unsatisfactory diagnosis being sudden death syndrome.

Jennifer Hennessey's ashes were scattered on the rear garden, her garden, and for the second time in his life Hennessey experienced the incongruence of a summer funeral. Summers, he had long held, are for weddings, good weather gives to a wedding, and in a similar way, winter weather gives to a funeral. Folk can choose one but not the other and for many years George Hennessey had hoped for an autumn or winter death. Upon grieving for his wife and picking up his life he had been set about devoting his spare time to landscaping the rear garden to Jennifer's design and some thirty years later the design had matured. That Jennifer's ashes were in the garden meant he could never leave the house and it had become his long established custom to talk to her, to tell her of the day he had had and of any developments in his life. Lately he had told her of a new love in his life but had assured her that his love for her had not at all diminished, in fact it had grown stronger, that a candle still burned for her, and in response he felt enveloped in a warmth which could not be explained by the sun's rays alone.

That evening he dined on a pair of grilled pork chops and vegetables and spent the rest of the evening sitting in his favourite chair reading an account of the battle of Waterloo, being a recent acquisition to his collection of military history. Later, Oscar having been fed, and the sun down, man and dog who loved each other, took their customary walk into the fields at the edge of Easingwold. One mile out, one mile back. Later still, Hennessey strolled into Easingwold, observing the small bats flitting and darting in the evening air. He went to the Dove Inn and had a pint, just one, before last orders were called.

Chapter Four

Saturday, 3rd of August
in which is met an enigmatic man and the gentle reader is privy to a crisis in Yellich's life.

"Try again," Yellich said.

"Try again. Harder." Hennessey echoed.

Hennessey and Yellich had arrived at Micklegate Bar Police Station at 8.30a.m., driving into the car park, one behind the other, and had walked side by side towards the rear Staff Only entrance, where Yellich paused, deferentially, to allow Hennessey to enter the building ahead of him. They signed in at the enquiry desk, checked their pigeonholes, sifting through circulars for any important messages, and then walked down the CID corridor, with Yellich peeling off to enter his office and Hennessey walking on a few feet to his. Moments later Yellich was sitting in front of Hennessey's desk cradling a steaming mug of tea in his hands.

"Can't think without it," he had said.

"First tea of the day…know what you mean," had been Hennessey's warm reply. "Well, walk or ride?"

"Well, a walk would be a gentle amble along the wall to Baile Hill and a little on the pavement after that but I think we ought to go by car, I think we'll be told of another address."

"I think we will be."

Fifteen minutes later they were in the cramped office of Walter Tamm, owner and managing director of Fashion on Long Close Lane. After the preliminaries, Tamm claimed not to know Luke Brogan of Liaisons fame.

"Try again," Yellich said.

"Try again. Harder." Hennessey echoed.

Walter Tamm eyed the cops with cold and undisguised distaste.

"The owner of the letting agency told us you know Luke Brogan."

"He's not the owner."

"Don't be evasive. We can do this at the police station or we can do it here," Hennessey snarled, "but we're going to do it."

"Arrest me? For what?"

"Obstruction." Hennessey held eye contact with Tamm.

"For a start," Yellich also held eye contact with Tamm, "and we could take a close look at your business."

"My business?"

"Your business...make sure all those designer clothes are what they seem to be...what you claim them to be."

Tamm paled. Already small, he seemed to shrink further.

"So co-operate. It's in your interest."

Tamm sank back in his chair. "Okay...I knew Brogan."

"Better."

"I said I knew him."

"Alright, so how did you know him?"

"Business."

"You were in business together?"

"No, I knew him through the business community in York...never close...only as Mr Brogan."

"Which is probably another lie," Hennessey growled.

Tamm glared at him.

"Mr Redfern of Malton and Pickering Lets informed us that you and Luke Brogan were on first name terms." Hennessey paused, then added "You've got snared up in your own lies, Mr Tamm. If you lie to police officers, you invite the dread finger of suspicion to point at you."

"I have nothing to hide from you."

"Pleased to hear it. So you don't mind if we do a bit of investigating?"

"About what?"

"About you...all about you."

"I haven't been in trouble with the law since I was fifteen."

"Yes we know, handling stolen goods...says a lot about you that, let other people do the stealing, let other people take the risk, buy shoplifted items at half their retail price."

"Got receipts for all the gear for sale out there?" Yellich asked. "I mean, if they are the real thing, doesn't mean to say you bought them from the approved wholesaler."

"What are you driving at?"

"Well, a small out-of-the-way shop like this, selling top of the range designer clothes..."

"So?"

"So...well, when we have this inquiry wrapped up and the felon who murdered Svetlana Zvonoreva is safely under lock and key..."

"Which will happen," Yellich smiled.

"We'll take a close look at your paperwork and check on any reports of designer clothing being stolen."

"That will happen too," Yellich continued to smile.

"Or we could forget about Svetlana Zvonoreva and since we are here, seize this golden opportunity to go over your files now."

"Which could easily happen." Yellich's smile turned into a grin.

"So where do we find Luke Brogan?"

"Seek him in the wind."

"You are not being very clever, Mr Tamm," Hennessey replied.

"It's a serious answer," Tamm shrugged. "It's just what Brogan is like, he just floats about, no specific direction...he'll appear and disappear, one underpaid job then a wild harebrained scheme to make a lot of money in a short space of time...which always fails."

"Like Liaisons?"

"Exactly. Then it's back to another underpaid bit of employment."

"Address?"

"Bedsit land."

"I see. What does he look like?"

"Tall, beard...ginger beard, sometimes it's long and straggly, sometimes it's trimmed short, depends on his status, his situation. If he's up to his business building it's trimmed, if he's unemployed or on the dole it's straggly."

"Do we know him?"

"I don't know...do you?" Tamm smiled at the cleverness of his retort.

"So how would we find him?"

"Beats me, he might not even be in York, he was talking of going to Thailand."

"Thailand!"

"Yes...he's mid thirties and likes them young, not criminally young, but in their teens still...as close to the age of consent the better. Thailand is a good place, he said once."

There was a lull in the conversation; it was broken by Yellich who asked, "You took over this shop from him?"

"Yes?"

"He must have left a forwarding address?"

Hennessey turned and nodded approvingly at Yellich.

Tamm looked stung.

"First name terms, Walter," Hennessey probed, "don't dig yourself any deeper."

"Well, he asked me to forward any mail to his father's address."

"Which is?"

Tamm reached sideways and opened a drawer in his desk and extracted an address book. As he did so, Yellich instinctively took his notebook from his jacket pocket.

"L Brogan," Tamm read, "Naseby Hall."

"Married." Hennessey commented.

"Yes, the old boy has money...in Long Fenton, that's a village in the Vale, so I believe."

"Naseby Hall, Long Fenton." Yellich wrote in his pad. "What does the *L* stand for?"

"Can't tell you. Luke I suppose...Luke senior, Luke junior. Why don't you ask him?"

"We will." Hennessey turned. "Don't worry, we will."

"I helped you, yes?"

"Yes..." Yellich also turned, "grudgingly...but you assisted."

"So I don't need to worry about a visit from you guys on another matter?"

Hennessey turned back and stared at Tamm who he saw had come to wear a smug expression. "Oh yes, Mr Tamm, no blind eyes are turned. If you've been up to no good, you have to worry a great deal about a visit from us guys about any other matter."

"But you said..."

"We said nothing," Yellich held open the door for Hennessey, "we made no promises. You might...you might have bought yourself a bit of time, but that's all."

Tamm paled.

Sitting in the passenger seat of the car, Hennessey consulted the road atlas.

"He's up to no good," Yellich mused as Hennessey turned the pages.

"Tamm? Yes, he's got something to hide."

"I'm going to crank up the pressure on him. He must have a warehouse somewhere."

"You haven't got enough for a warrant to permit you to search it."

"Not yet," Yellich replied grimly. "Not yet."

"Hello..."

What's that boss?"

"Long Fenton."

"You've found it?"

"Yes...and it's very close to the stretch of water called Stillwater Lake."

"Well, indeed." Yellich turned the ignition key, "and what do you think *L* stands for?"

"Leo." Hennessey closed the road atlas. "I have an inkling that it will stand for Leo."

"So have I, skipper. So have I."

Yellich drove out of York and into the Vale, green and yellow fields of plenty under a blue sky. He followed Hennessey's directions to Long Fenton and an enquiry of a postman, clearly near the end of his round by the empty nature of his sack, brought forth precise directions to Naseby Hall.

Naseby Hall stood beyond the village proper, separated from the cottages by two large fields, so Hennessey noted. The estate itself was bounded by metal fencing, the horizontal fencing was cylindrical in cross section, and attached to rectangular uprights which were placed at six feet intervals, the fence itself being about four foot high and painted entirely black. A line of trees; beech, horse chestnut and oak had been planted inside the metal fence and looked to Hennessey's untrained eye to be about two hundred years old and had probably been planted when the fence was installed. It may well, he thought, have been the thinking that the fence would be a temporary measure to be used until the trees grew to their magnificence to act as a more permanent boundary marker of the lands of Naseby Hall. It was a testament to the skill of the metal wrights of the late eighteenth or early nineteenth century, Hennessey pondered, that the metal fence was still wholly visible. The gateway was stone, two massive vertical columns of Yorkshire stone, perhaps twelve foot high, and Hennessey knew with at least the same amount below the surface to ensure stability. On one stone column was engraved with the word 'Naseby' and the other, the right one, was engraved with the word 'Hall'. Both words had been freshly picked out in white paint.

"Nice," Yellich said as he halted the car in front of the gateway, the gates of which had been removed, "and not frightened of visitors either...I mean, no gates."

"Yes, but let's not read too much into that, let's see what we see." Hennessey wiped his brow. He had noticed before how much more, noticeably more, he perspired in the heat than did the younger Yellich.

Yellich drove slowly up the gravel driveway, the car tyres crunching the gravel alerted a springer spaniel and three mongrels who burst from the shrubs near the house barking in alarm. Yellich halted the car beside a Riley RMA green and black, circa 1950, graceful lines, running boards.

"Like Dr D'Acre's," Yellich commented.

"Just as I was thinking," Hennessey replied, studying the mongrel, which had stationed itself at his side of the car and knowing dogs, he decided the animal was all bark and no bite. "I confess, I prefer the red and white of Dr D'Acre's Riley to the black and green of that one." He also confessed privately that he might take a shine to the owner of Naseby Hall whose dogs were soft mouthed gun dogs, for the mongrels were of that line, looking like Hennessey's beloved Oscar, akin to a scaled down Labrador. He would have liked the owner of Naseby Hall much less, even prior to meeting him, had, for example, his house been guarded by a pack of snarling Dobermans. He turned to Yellich, "I think it's safe." He opened the car door and stepped out. The mongrel backed off a little but continued barking.

"How is it they pick on me?" Yellich smiled and he too left the car. "I've got two to contend with, you've only got one."

"Take it as a compliment, Yellich. They find you more attractive."

The two officers walked past the old Riley and up a short flight of steps to the green painted door of Naseby Hall. Hennessey reached for an iron ring set in the stone doorway and pulled it. Bells were heard jingling within the building. As they waited for the door to be answered, the two officers looked around them. Yellich noticed well-tended gardens, not so well tended as to merit the description of them being 'manicured', nor were they elaborately landscaped. The garden design, he thought, could be described as 'sensible', a lawn in front of the house, shrubs to the side, one man with power tools could keep the garden from becoming wild and impossibly overgrown. Quite a pleasant location too, deep in the Vale, a cool summer's day, a little breeze, not overbearingly hot, and three dogs for company. He imagined a pleasant day's work in cutting the lawn and the shrubs and then having carried the cuttings to a pile to be left to dry before being burned, a wash and a change of clothing and a stroll into Church Fenton feeling the sense of satisfaction that a day's labouring can bring, and the well earned beer and game of dominoes, a stroll back to enjoy the sleep of the just.

Hennessey on the other hand pondered the building.

The date 1790 made the building about the vintage he had suspected by the age of the metal boundary fencing and the age of the trees within the fencing, all in a row, and thus clearly planted by a human hand. The frontage of the building was tall and narrow. Either side of the door were two sash windows; above the door on the first floor, was a sash window with two sash windows on either side, and similarly above that, five sash windows, then there would doubtless be an attic, a house of three storeys; ground, first and second plus attic. He doubted it would be more than two rooms deep and was thus a tall house, rather than squat and broad. Hennessey noticed outbuildings to the right of his vantage point, and looked out over the lawn to the fencing, which at that point on its length wasn't with the accompaniment of trees, to the rolling country beyond, noticing how two small woods stood at either side of an uninterrupted view of what was by British standards a very distant skyline. It was more than likely, he thought, having read widely upon the subject of British history, that the centre of the wood had been felled and cleared to provide that vista. Most probably when the house was built. The name too, clearly drawn from the battle of Naseby which he well knew was a parliamentarian victory in the English Civil War and where a man called Cromwell first came to the good notice of his peers, and yet the house was clearly built after the restoration of the monarchy. Calling a house 'Naseby' in 1790 was, he thought, an insensitive gesture. The poorest people in the Vale were by then faring much worse than they had fared under Charles II and his Royal predecessors. The peasants had lost the protection of the Star Chamber with which they could challenge the landowners, and with Parliamentarianism had come enforced enclosures of the fields into single units, and the bitterly contested loss of common lands. Similarly, the ancient right to take fish from the river or fowl from the air became a crime; even picking up a faggot of wood with which to light a fire in a cottage hearth upon a winter's night, was deemed theft. After the establishment of Parliament, all lands were owned by the landowner, and he owned all things upon that land whether living or dead. The landless worked for a wage and the penalties in 1790 were Draconian for taking anything from the land with which to supplement the meagre wage. Insensitive, or wilfully cruel in its mocking of the landless, Hennessey again felt that naming a house in 1790 in honour of a Parliamentary victory was, as might be said in the early twenty-first century, 'politically incorrect'.

Hennessey reached for the bell pull to give a second ring when the door opened. The man opened the door slowly, on his terms, looked at Hennessey and then Yellich, and then back to Hennessey. Clearly it seemed to the officers that he assumed, correctly so, that the elder man was also the senior in terms of rank. He remained silent but his countenance was warm and welcoming.

"Police," Hennessey said.

"Yes, I gathered." Then turned to the dogs and said, "Hush!" The dogs fell silent but continued to eye Hennessey and Yellich with suspicion.

"How so?"

"Your manner, your dress, your air of confident authority and you don't look like burglars pretending to be double glazing salesman in order to 'sight up' my home and check my security arrangements. How can I help you?"

"You are Mr L Brogan?"

"I am he." Brogan was a man in his sixties. He was, like Hennessey, also silver haired, but unlike Hennessey, seemed thin, gaunt."

"We are really trying to trace one Luke Brogan, we believe he is your son?"

"Luke, yes..."

"Where can we find him?"

Brogan hesitated. "For that information, I will have to see some identification, please."

The cops flashed their IDs.

"Well, he's not here..."

"He lives here?"

"On and off. We have a house, a small cottage, he is renovating it. He may be there now, he may not, but that's Luke. He comes and goes when it pleases him."

"Where is the cottage?"

"In Long Fenton," Brogan pointed back towards the village, "more or less on the other side from here. Has the original name of E.W.E., Cottage."

"Yew?" Hennessey asked. "As in the tree?"

"No, ewe as in the sheep, e.w.e., believed to have been a shepherd's cottage in ancient times, so the story goes. We've had the cottage a while, it's a bit untidy, Luke is fixing it up, hopes to sell it."

"I see. Can I ask what your Christian name is, sir?"

"Mine?"

"Yes, yours."

"Leonard. I am Leonard Brogan...my son is Luke."

"Leonard," Hennessey echoed, "sometimes shortened to Leo?"

Brogan paused; he looked stung. Hennessey's interest in Leonard Brogan was suddenly increased, as was Yellich's. "Sometimes," Brogan whispered. "Yes, I have been called Leo on occasions."

"I see. I wonder if we might come inside, sir? We have a few questions for you."

"For me? I thought you were looking for Luke? Mind you, what for I don't know – he's a good boy."

"I am sure he is, but may we come in?"

"Of course, please..." Brogan stepped aside looking cool in a blue short-sleeved shirt, white slacks, and lightweight leather sandals. The only decoration that Hennessey and Yellich noted was a functional looking watch.

Brogan led Hennessey and Yellich to a room at the back of the house. Two tall windows looked out onto an extensive lawn bounded by a high brick wall. Inside the room was simply but tastefully decorated: old but solid looking furniture, deep armchairs, two settees, an oak table; oil paintings in frames hung on the wall. The room was dark and cool.

"North facing..." Brogan said, "always a cool room, damned cold in the winter though, too damned cold, but summers on days like this, this is the room to be in." A copy of the *Yorkshire Post* lay open at the crossword page. Brogan noticed Hennessey glance at it. "Yes, I was attempting the crossword when you called. Please," Brogan indicated the chairs and settees, "please take a seat."

Hennessey and Yellich sat. Hennessey chose a chair; Yellich more modestly sat on the settee, further from Brogan than was Hennessey. Brogan sat, he too in an armchair, his back to the window.

"A large house, Mr Brogan?"

"Yes, it's lovely, isn't it? Quite old...you will have noticed the date above the door?"

"Yes...impressive."

"Well, it has been well maintained and modernised, a Victorian range in the kitchen...electric lighting, as you see." He looked upwards. Hennessey followed his gaze and saw light bulbs hanging in ornamental shades. "And running water and flushing toilets."

"Big garden...do you manage that yourself, Mr Brogan?"

"Heavens, no," Brogan smiled, "the gardening is contracted out."

"You and your wife?" Hennessey indicated a photograph of a middle aged couple which stood on the mantel-piece.

"No, me and my twin sister on our sixtieth birthday. My wife died."

"I am sorry. I understand the loss."

"You do, Mr...?"

"Hennessey. Yes, I am a widower."

"Well, it may well be that your loss was greater than mine. Sylvia and I were estranged, fully divorced, and had been for nearly twenty years by then, so the sense of loss was not as great as it could be. The only sadness is that she had a relatively short life by western standards, only fifty-two when cancer took her."

"I see..." Hennessey paused. The questions would be asked, and asked soon, but the rapport was, he felt, passing useful in respect of a man who seemed to have something to hide when he was asked if he was a.k.a. Leo. "The phrase you just used...by western standards, is interesting. I confess that most folk would complain that fifty-two was an early age to die of natural causes but globally speaking it's quite a respectable age." Hennessey genuinely liked Leonard Brogan for the sentiment he had expressed. He thought it spoke of an unselfish and a grateful mind.

"Well... probably I am out of kilter with most folk in the West having lived a lot of my life in the third world. I have seen dreadful poverty and widespread infant mortality, so I suppose that had shaped my attitude."

"I see." The explanation made sense but it still meant in Hennessey's view, that Brogan was a man of generous spirit. He felt it made the possibility that he had something to hide, and that he may be implicated in the death of a Russian exchange student, all the more puzzling. But this was early days, still very early days. He asked what Brogan had been doing in the developing world.

"Cultivating marginal land, developing disease resistant crops, advising on methods of increasing yield...that sort of thing. I am a biologist. The plant world is fascinating, Mr Hennessey, much more varied than the animal kingdom and much more vicious."

"Vicious?" Hennessey looked at the window at the neatly kept lawn surrounded by flowerbeds that was the rear garden of Naseby Hall, and he thought of his own back garden in Easingwold...in the two gardens he sensed only tranquillity.

"Vicious," Brogan smiled. "A garden is a never-ending battleground and to fight that, plant species have to seek domination and hence survival. Heavens, it makes any fight between animals look like a Sunday School picnic. Seeing a garden as a place of peace and contentment, or a forest as a place of calm mysticism is human naïvety, dreadful battles are being waged and it never stops. If you left your garden to its own devices the grasses would dominate. That closely cut lawn out there is in fact the dominant plant. If it was allowed to do so, it would suffocate all other small plants."

"Suffocate?"

"Smother...cover from sunlight. Only the trees could survive the grass, but they would go very thirsty, grass has a vicious thirst. It would suck up most all rainfall before it seeped down low enough to top up the water table and thus enable the trees to drink."

"Fascinating."

"It is really," Brogan smiled, "but you didn't come to talk to me about plants."

"No, no, we didn't." Hennessey shifted his position in the chair. He sensed Yellich tense. "It's in connection with a murdered girl."

"A murdered girl?"

"You will have read the news. I see the *Post* beside you.

I am sure you had it delivered for more than the cross-word."

"I walk into the village and buy it, it's my daily exercise, but yes, I read the news, national and regional."

"You will doubtless have read about the murdered Russian student?"

"Oh my, yes, found quite close to here...by Stillwater Lake."

"Yes...that's the one."

"Astounding story... frozen."

"Yes. She was in possession of a book of matches..."

"I read she was naked."

"Oh, she was. The lady who let her a room was good enough, foresighted enough, to keep her possessions."

"Ah..."

"Yes, she realised some ill must have come of her and kept all her possessions. She hadn't a great deal...came into this life with nothing."

"As we all do."

"Left with nothing."

"As again, we all do."

"Indeed, but in the interim she accumulated little...though she hadn't much opportunity...little opportunity to acquire wealth and possessions even in post-Communist Russia, and given that she was iced at the tender age of nineteen, well..."

"I see what you mean. Yes, unlike the lucky ones who accumulate well..." Brogan glanced about him. "Naseby Hall isn't as grand as it looks, but yes, I count myself lucky to own her." Brogan paused. "The house has a distinct atmosphere, it has character, it's warm and welcoming. I sensed it as soon as I crossed the threshold when I first viewed her, when she was up for sale. I thought 'I must have this house,' and offered generously...it has, well, it's a 'she', not a 'he' of a building...definitely not an 'it'. I am a lucky man to own 'her', but she's not as valuable as you might think, she's prone to flooding. This part of the Vale is very low-lying, I can't get insurance against flood damage...that reduces the value considerably."

"I imagine."

"Then above, the rooms are fairly spartan in terms of their decoration, there's nothing valuable in the house. Met a man once, loudmouth, boorish businessman, owned property in a very prestigious part of Sheffield and boasted that the contents of his house were worth more than the building. Alas, I can't say that, not sure I would want to...the more you have, the more you can lose. I am comfortable with my lot...oh...and the central heating is turned down to conserve fuel. In winter we wrap up, we sit here in heavy pullovers and scarves, woolly hats and heavy woollen hiking socks but it's fun...we joke about it."

"We?"

"Oh, yes, sometimes Luke is here and sometimes I offer accommodation."

"To whom?"

"To those who need it."

"Like?"

"Well, the vulnerable people who probably wouldn't survive the winter...only one or two...I think the Hall enjoys being used like that."

Hennessey didn't comment, a building having a "presence" as in a ghost he could understand, having not been without the occasional psychic experience, but bricks and mortar and slate having a soul? There he and Brogan parted company.

"Well," Hennessey brought the conversation back on track. "The murdered girl was in possession of a book of matches..."

"You said, yes."

"Had the name Leo written inside."

"And you are pointing the accusing finger at me out of all the other Leo's in the United Kingdom?" Brogan inclined his head to one side and smiled.

"Not at all." Hennessey returned the smile. "We are not pointing the accusing finger at anyone...not yet."

"Not yet," Brogan echoed. "You are a confident man, Mr Hennessey."

"Well, I don't know about that, but I am an old copper...and in my old copper's waters I feel success in this case; this case will have an early and successful closure."

"Despite what you say, I still sense confidence from you."

"I hope you are right. But your son, Luke...once owned a business venture called Liaisons."

"Yes."

"A dating agency."

"Yes. Luke has been spectacularly unsuccessful in his life, it saddens me to say...blood is blood...he has proved a disappointment to me, he is my only child, he has started many business ventures, none have succeeded, Liaisons being one."

"The point being, that we believe the Russian girl registered with Liaisons."

"Yes? So did a few other women, and that I understand was Luke's problem. What registration he had was imbalanced, grossly so, ten men for every female. Despite the name of the company, he just couldn't make the liaisons."

"I see, but there is the link..."

"Link?"

"The girl is linked to Liaisons, the proprietor of Liaisons was your son, Luke, and the book of matches was found in Svetlana Zvanoreva's possession."

"Oh..." Brogan groaned. "Please, for your own sake, Mr Hennessey, for the sake of your professional credibility, I counsel you not to make links where no link exists. That sort of thinking would not impress a lawyer."

"Long way to go before we submit anything to the CPS, Mr Brogan. Perhaps 'lead' is a better word than 'link'."

"Lead...link...still very tenuous."

"Can I ask you a straight and simple question, Mr Brogan?"

"Certainly."

"Did you ever meet Svetlana Zvonoreva?"

"No." Brogan held eye contact with Hennessey. "I can look you in the eye and say truthfully that I have not, did not, ever meet her."

"Thanks." Hennessey smiled. He was beginning to sense Brogan to be a truthful man...yet...yet...yet...a suspicion about the man nagged at him. The man seemed warm and genuine, but all too often he had seen the darker side of individuals emerge. He had seen how warm and genuine people can also reveal themselves to be cold and disingenuous. He had to concede though, that the link between Brogan and the matches found amongst Svetlana Zvonoreva's possessions was, at best, tenuous in the extreme, at worst, it was nonexistent. He looked at Brogan and asked, "Do you possess a deep freeze?" Brogan looked startled by the question and Hennessey, the old copper, with the waters of an old copper, felt that he had touched a raw nerve and suspicion once again focused on Brogan. "Can we see it, please?"

"If you wish." Brogan stood, revealing himself to seem quite frail and unsteady on his feet, as if old for his age, so Hennessey thought, as he, possibly only a few years younger than Brogan, stood strongly and steadily and similarly, Yellich proved himself to be youthful and lithe.

Brogan led the officers through Naseby Hall, down a long corridor which was tall, yet narrow. Hennessey thought that the corridor offered the vertical space to allow one man to stand on another's shoulders, but two men would have to give way to each other if they wished to pass each other. The corridor gave way to the kitchen, in which a large, gas-fired range stood against the further wall, and a solid table occupied the greater part of the floor space; working surfaces and cupboards were noted by the two officers, as were many utensils hanging from hooks on the wall. The officers were led through the kitchen to a doorway, which led into a scullery; a second doorway opened to the outside and beyond a gravelled area, a number of out-buildings. As the men's feet crunched the gravel, the dogs barked and ran to investigate the sound. "Alright!" Brogan held up his hand and the dogs stopped barking but eyed Hennessey and Yellich curiously. "Gravel," Brogan smiled as he opened the door of one of the outbuildings, "best anti-burglar device you can get…that and a couple of dogs."

"So we noticed when we arrived." Hennessey noticed that there were by then four dogs, the original three having been joined by a fourth black mongrel. It seemed similar to a dog Hennessey remembered from somewhere, but couldn't place.

"Yes…never been burgled." Brogan pushed the door open, and he and Yellich and Hennessey stepped gratefully into the cool and shade of the building. "This…" he stood in front of a long, white metal container, "this is the deep freeze."

"Quite large," Hennessey observed.

"Yes…the sort used in hotels and hospitals."

"And prisons," Hennessey added and Brogan shot a glance towards him. "Seems to upset you, Mr Brogan?"

"What does?"

"The mention of prison."

"Didn't intend to give that impression."

"But you did." Once again, Hennessey found his suspicion rising in respect of Brogan; he was puzzled how he could find the man truthful and also suspicious by turns.

"Don't read too much into it...into my mannerism." He opened the lid of the deep freeze, using both hands, and Hennessey saw how the man who looked weak when standing, could summon strength once he had found his feet. Hennessey and Yellich glanced into the deep freeze. It contained food items and nothing else. It was as the officers had expected, but in addition, they saw what they were looking for. The length of the deep freeze could easily accommodate the short and slight frame of Svetlana Zvonoreva. Nor was it lost on Hennessey and Yellich that the woodland in which her body was discovered was probably no more than five minutes drive from Naseby Hall.

"Is everything alright, Leo?"

The three men turned to the door. The owner of the voice was a small, slightly built young female. She looked at Hennessey and said, "You..." in a near accusing tone.

"Well well well." Hennessey found it hard to conceal his own surprise. "We meet yet again...such a small world."

"Yeah." Speake shrugged.

"Thought I recognised the dog from somewhere."

"Yeah...Leo's looking after it while I work."

"Work?" Hennessey raised his eyebrows. "Begging is hardly work..."

"It brings in money."

"You two evidently know each other." Brogan shut the deep freeze.

"Yes." Hennessey's suspicion once again fell on Brogan, the shutting of the lid of the deep freeze seemed to him to be a little too eager for a man with nothing to hide. "Yes..."

he repeated. "Emily and I have met. Can I ask what you are doing here?"

"I live here."

Hennessey glanced at Brogan.

"I have a large house, I see nothing wrong in offering temporary accommodation to vulnerable people."

"Very charitable of you," Hennessey said.

"Very noble," Yellich added.

"It's just until they are ready to move on."

"I see." Hennessey looked from Emily Speake to Brogan and back to Emily Speake. He saw two needy people, the waiflike Emily and Brogan, with his attitude of compulsive rescuer. "But your charity doesn't stop you allowing Naseby Hall to be used as a base for begging?"

Brogan looked disapprovingly at Emily Speake, who looked away from his gaze.

"It's still better than what she was doing when I found her."

"Which was?"

"Living in a hide in the woods by Stillwater Lake, living off berries...and that was spring time, still cold then...I brought her back here."

"What were you doing in the woods?"

"Walking the dogs...the grounds are large, as you see, but they enjoy and deserve a change of scenery, so one or twice a week in the mornings, when it's safer, the least risky time..."

"Risky?"

"Less risk of burglary."

"Yes..." It was, he conceded, a fair point, the chances of being burgled increased from ten a.m. onwards, peaking at about three p.m. From six p.m. to ten a.m. there is a lull, as the felons rest. So police statistics have shown.

"So, I brought her back here and she has been here

for...well, since spring." He addressed Emily Speake. "Not happy with your begging though. I'm sorry to hear that."

Emily Speake shrugged.

"It was my understanding that Emily was going into York for more positive reasons," Brogan turned to Hennessey, "looking for work and accommodation."

"I see...well, it's not really my concern...my interest lies elsewhere."

"Yes..."

"Do many...many..." Hennessey struggled to find the correct words, the Victorianism 'unfortunates' came rapidly to his mind, but he declined to use it, "many vulnerable people live with you?"

"Never more than two at a time. I want to do what I can, but I am careful not to lose control of my house. At the moment, Emily is my only guest...and nothing untoward happens...she has her own room with a solid bolt on the inside."

"That's true." Emily Speake spoke with a frail voice. "I just have to keep clean."

"My only stipulation," Brogan said. "A bath upon arrival and all clothing thoroughly washed. Oh...and when here, they keep out of trouble with you gentlemen."

"Yes," Emily Speake spoke in support of Leo Brogan. "Leo's strict on that point."

"Which is why I am disappointed to find out you have been begging. We'll talk about that later."

Driving back to York, Hennessey broke the silence, and from the front passenger seat asked, "Impressions?"

"Of Brogan?" Yellich kept his eyes focused on the road and drove at a steady forty miles an hour. Two cars were close behind, clearly impatient for an increase in speed, but that section of the road was narrow and heavy with oncoming traffic. Overtaking was not possible and Yellich wasn't going to be intimidated, so forty mph it was.

"Of anything and anyone." Hennessey glanced to his left. For personal reasons, he disliked driving, he had always failed to see the attraction of cars and motorcycles, particularly the latter. Couldn't understand why people, particularly young men, wanted to possess one, viewing them as he did, as the most dangerous machine ever invented, whether two wheels or four. He was also content to leave the stress and road rage to others. The second advantage that he found in not driving, unless he couldn't avoid doing so, was that being a passenger afforded more time for observation. How fortunate he was that he was able to turn his head from side to side, though in the main he looked to his left to enjoy the vista of the Vale in high summer, the flat, slightly rolling landscape, the roof tops of a distant hamlet, the rich fields dotted here and there with areas of mixed woodland, all under a vast, and on that day, blue and near cloudless sky. Hennessey thought himself fortunate to be able to absorb the pleasing image of rural Yorkshire whilst Yellich, poor Yellich, was obliged to keep his sight fixed firmly ahead, with the occasional glance in the rear view mirror, and maintain a high level of concentration throughout. "You could start with Brogan, if you like."

"Could start with the deep freeze. We both thought the same thing, skipper. Enough room to lay out the Russian student...she wasn't a big lassie. And by Brogan's own admission, the woods by Stillwater Lake are only five minutes away by car. And we know the body hadn't travelled far before it was dumped...it hadn't thawed. Not a lot of people live out that way, not many industrial sized deep freezers around...most others, all others, will be small, domestic appliances...smaller than a fridge."

"Point..." Hennessey's eye was caught by a pheasant standing in a meadow. He thought the bird looked bemused. It was just the image he caught as the car passed.

"Brogan himself..." Yellich shrugged his shoulders. "Queer bird...I mean, taking in waifs and strays...enjoying his dogs' company, living alone in that huge house...not a well man."

"You don't think so?"

"Well I'm no medical person, but he doesn't seem to have the physique to be able to tolerate working in the developing world for months on end...then a break to come home and then out to the tropics again...that takes stamina and you saw how he stood...very insecure in respect of his balance...though he had upper body strength. Lifted the lid of the deep freeze without any trouble."

"Yes, I noticed that."

"But taking in waifs and strays...that's sentimental, slushy do-gooding. Once knew a lady, a Quaker lady, filled her house with tramps because she believed it was her Christian duty...Quakers are very big minded folk...but that, I thought, was verging on certifiable insanity."

"Your point?"

"Well...my point, boss, is that opening doors to the least and most needful amongst us is not unknown, but I cannot see a person who does that also murdering some-one...keeping their body on ice for three years and then carrying it out and dumping it in woodland, clearly hoping it won't be found. Not for a while, anyway."

"Not be found?"

"Well, those woods are dense...no pathways."

"Yes...I was forgetting it was only a twitcher looking to spy on a nesting pair of lesser spotted great bustard..."

"Kites, boss, he was wanting to look at red kites. Anyway, the bustard became extinct in the nineteenth century." Yellich smiled.

"Ah…but as you say…murder…she was struck on the back of the head, kept for three years and then disposed of in thick woodland. If it wasn't for that twitcher, she would still be there…beginning to decompose in this heat, could be years before she was found…but a callous act like that just doesn't sit well with the character of a man who offers his home to the likes of Miss Speake."

"That was the girl?"

"Yes…spoke to her in York a couple of times. First time she was sitting begging in the sun and her black dog was suffering dreadfully in the heat…bought the dog some water and told her to move on."

"Good of you, boss." Again Yellich smiled.

"Any dog lover would have done the same. Anyway, went back a little later…after lunch that day, and she'd moved on. Saw her a day or two later, heading for the touristy bits of the city. On that occasion she was without the dog, said she had left it with someone who'd look after it."

"Now we know who."

"Indeed…" Hennessey glanced out across a yellow field of oil seed. "Indeed, we do."

"Think she's involved? The lassie Speake, I mean?"

"Can't see it somehow…she's spaced out from all that heroin…still in the clouds…she won't do anything with her life until she's got her feet on the ground."

"Doesn't mean to say she didn't see or hear anything, boss."

"Doesn't, does it?" Hennessey turned briefly to Yellich, then returned his gaze to the patchwork of fields.

"And you know, I think you touched a raw nerve or two back there."

"Yes, I saw him twitch and start at the mention of

prison, and he seemed to jump when I mentioned a deep freeze."

"Yes, I picked that up as well, boss."

"So, what points to him?"

"Well..." Yellich paused, "not in any order of priority...just a little brainstorm..."

"Understood."

"The proximity of the woods, just five minutes by car, as we have said."

"Yes."

"And he knows the woods, he exercises his dogs there."

"Strange place to exercise dogs...no pathways."

"There are pathways...the body was dumped in a part of the wood where the vegetation is particularly dense and isn't penetrated by pathways, it's about one hundred yards thick and about the same deep, it extends from near the road to the water's edge. The path through the wood skirts round it and runs near the road but that is what is meant by the wood having no pathways. A section of 100 yards square, or about 100 metres, has no pathway."

"I see."

"But a man who exercises his dogs there would know of that stand of vegetation."

"Okay."

"He's in possession of a deep freeze, large enough to contain the body of Svetlana Zvonoreva, and, as we have said..."

"Yes."

"His name, Leonard, known as Leo, is the same name as on the book of matches."

"Yes."

"There's the Liaisons connection. Desperate to find the Englishman of her dreams she joins Liaisons which is, or was, run by Brogan the younger."

"Yes...this is good."

"Well, that's about it. Can't think of anything else that points to him."

"Very well. So...the balance."

"The balance, skipper?"

"Yes...hate rushing in. So, what points away from him? I mean, what points to his not being involved in this murder?"

"Well..." Yellich slowed to allow an impatient motorcyclist to squeeze narrowly between him and an oncoming bus. As he did so, Hennessey was reminded of the reason for his dislike, nay loathing, of motor vehicles. "Frankly, as much as points to him being involved..."

"Go on."

"Lack of motivation...massive age gap. I can't see a man in his sixties getting involved with a nineteen year old to the extent that passion was involved between them. And passion was involved because the body was concealed for such a length of time. She definitely had some involvement with her killer for that to have happened."

"Yes, good point."

"And, as we have also said, the manner of the man, gives his life to developing marginalized agriculture in the third world, and something else..."

"Disease resistant crops?"

"That's it...and his way of taking in the likes of Miss Speake, that's not a man who murders viciously and hides a body for three years and then leaves it where he hopes it will decompose into nothing and not be found at all."

"So, on balance...all in all?"

"On balance, not a nice man...cagey...needs a closer look. He's got a side to him...but the way in is the Speake girl."

"How do you suggest we handle it?"

"I think we lift her when she comes into the famous and faire with her begging bowl. We can do that tomorrow, sir. She'll come in on Sunday if this weather holds."

"Don't you have this Sunday off?"

"For this..." Yellich slowed as they approached the houses which were the outskirts of York, "for this, I'll come in. Sara won't like it...but...she shouldn't have married a cop." He paused. "I'm not really that chauvinistic."

"I didn't think you were, Yellich. Seriously."

"I'll come in but I'll pay for it," he grinned, "Sara will extract her pound of flesh."

Yellich drove home to Huntingdon on the outskirts of York. He drove to a newly built housing estate and drew up at the kerb beside a modest house with a small lawn to the front, which served to separate the house from the pavement. The house seemed quiet...too quiet...and Yellich sensed something amiss. There was no sign of anything wrong, the house looked as it always looked, neatly kept, clean, no different from houses on either side of it or opposite it. There was though, no movement, no opening of the door upon his arrival, no Jeremy bounding out of the house, arms outstretched, to greet him, no Sara at the kitchen, smiling her welcome. Yellich got out of the car, and locking it, leaving one window slightly open so the interior of the car could 'breathe' in the heat. Carrying his jacket underarm, he walked with growing curiosity up the driveway to the front door. Still no response from inside the house. He took his key, unlocked the door and stepped over the threshold. "Hello..." he called out.

"Somerled!" The female voice came from the sitting room.

"Vicky?" Somerled Yellich recognised the voice of their

neighbour. He stepped into the living room as Victoria Sherman, slightly older than Somerled and Sara Yellich, stood to meet him. "Thank God you're home."

"What's happened?"

"It's Sara..."

"What's happened? Is she ill?"

"Probably."

"What do you mean? Where's Jeremy?"

"In our house, with my husband. It all happened about an hour ago..."

"What did?" Yellich didn't try to conceal the alarm in his voice. His legs felt weak, his stomach hollow.

"She came to our door...she was in a dreadful state...she had Jeremy...she pushed him into our house and said, 'Take him...Take him'."

"Oh...no," Yellich sat on the arm of a chair, "this has been brewing."

"Well, William...he was brilliant...lovely William, he saw what was happening and invited Jeremy upstairs to play with the train set...that's where they are now. You know how much Jeremy loves the toy train...mind, don't let William hear you describing it as a toy...he takes modelling seriously."

"Yes...yes."

"Anyway, as soon as Jeremy was out of earshot, poor Sara, she just collapsed in floods of tears. I thought it better if we came back here, got her away from Jeremy, got her into familiar surroundings. I know how children can be difficult...and Sara's by herself with Jeremy all day in the summer."

"Where is she?"

"I don't know...Sara...she just sat on the sofa and wept and wept. I wanted to phone you..."

"You should have."

"Sara wouldn't have it and she was still aware enough of things for me to say, 'Well, you're the boss'."

"Still...but alright, what happened?"

"She ran out of the house...she realised you must be on your way home and she just ran."

"Why...I wouldn't have harmed her?"

"It's not that...she knows that. I think it's because she didn't want you to see her like that."

"Where did she go?"

"I don't know...this was about half an hour ago."

"You should have phoned 999."

"I didn't get the impression she was going to harm herself...she just couldn't cope and has reached breaking point...she wants to collect herself."

"And you know that, do you?" Yellich stood angrily.

"Frankly, yes." Victoria Sherman allowed her voice to raise. "Yes...I do...as one woman who understands another, as someone who has been where Sara is now. My children didn't have Jeremy's condition, but they've all been five years old. Poor Sara has a twelve year old five year old...it's summer...he gets bored...he gets fractious...and he's probably just as strong as she is. He's certainly nearly as tall. She can't control him and he finally got on top of her."

"Oh..."

"Had it happened earlier in the day, I would have called you, but knowing you were coming home...I stayed. I don't have the keys to lock your house and I couldn't just pull the barrel lock behind me. There's been burglaries on the estate, even police officers' houses are not immune, so I remained here. I knew you wouldn't be long."

"Alright...thanks, Vicky. Is Jeremy alright where he is, with William?"

"I'm sure he'll be okay. Jeremy is quite captivated by the train set, and William loves playing with it."

"It might be another hour or so…I think I know where she's gone."

"That'll be alright. If there's anything we can do, Somerled…" Yellich smiled and nodded. "You've done a lot already. Thanks."

Yellich locked the house and walked purposefully, though refrained from running, out of the Huntingdon estate, to Church Lane, which ran straight into the fields driving towards a farm and the church of All Saints. It was in the grounds of the church of All Saints that Sara Yellich had been found once before in a tearful state, explaining as soon as she could that she loved the tranquillity of the churchyard.

Yellich walked into the Old Village and opposite the Blacksmith's Arms he turned down a narrow metalled sur-face pathway with neat houses with neat gardens to his right and a stable and paddock to his left, in which, as he passed, stood a white mare with her foal. As he approached the bridge over the river he heard a train in the distance, travelling at speed. He crossed the narrow river as it snaked its way through meadow and woodland, and entered the churchyard of All Saints Church, with the slate grey church with its somewhat stubby tower, topped by a gold painted weather vane in the outline of a cockerel. Yellich found Sara where he expected to find her, sitting by the memorial to the lost sons of the village. He recalled how they had once walked round the churchyard when newly arrived in Huntingdon and Sara had commented how unusual the war memorial was in that, unlike all other war memorials she had read, the Huntingdon memorial showed a similar num-ber of men lost in both wars, 'thirty to the Great War of 1914-1918, and 27 to the 1939-1945 war'. All other stones she had read recorded significantly more men lost from each locality to the first conflict. Yellich, in response, had offered by reason of explanation that the village had most likely expanded between the wars, moving from being a farming community is 1918, to a dormitory village of York, as suggested by the houses in the Old Village, which were clearly built in the 1920s and 1930s. Proportionally, therefore, thirty men lost to the 1914-1918 war would have represented a much greater loss of life than the losses to the 1939-1945 conflict. She had looked at him with distended eyes, a smile and a nod, as if to say, 'Yes, that makes sense'.

As Yellich approached her, she glanced up at him and smiled and ran her hand through her short, close cropped hair. He sat down next to her. He didn't speak and a pause developed. It grew into a silence, a silence in which the two, husband and wife for fourteen years, communicated, understanding each other perfectly.

"This is getting to be a habit." Sara Yellich turned to her husband and forced a smile.

Yellich returned the smile and took her hand. "Well, if it is, I'll know where to find you."

"Is Jeremy safe?"

"I haven't seen him, but I am assured he's playing with William Sherman's train set, not by himself, of course, William is with him."

"I'm sure he is." Sara sniffed and then said, "I'm sorry...I'm sorry...I'm..." And once again, burst into a fit of uncontrollable weeping, eventually managing to say. "I can't cope with him anymore, Somerled, he's getting too much. The summer is just going on, there's no end to it...he doesn't return to school until September, it's too long...my head's going to explode."

He slipped his arm round her slender shoulders and pulled her towards him, and she wept until his shirt was saturated.

"But I love him so..." she managed to say, "so, so much."

"I know," Yellich squeezed her shoulder gently, "I know. I know. He is born to be different and gives us so much...so much love...so much trust." He paused. "Perhaps your mother might help?"

"How?" She turned to him. "She couldn't take him."

"I was thinking she might move in...share the burden."

"You'd let her stay? You and she..."

"Well, I think for Jeremy's sake, she and I could...I don't know...agree to disagree. She can have the spare room...until school term starts...and when I get a day off, you and she could go away together, you would get a complete break."

"That would be great," she took his hand and squeezed it, "really great."

"I'll look after him for the rest of the day...you can phone your mother, she'll be able to get here tomorrow."

"From Northallerton? She could get here in an hour..."

"Well, phone her," Yellich stood and helped his wife to her feet, "whatever you wish."

"Alright. I'll ask mum to keep out of your way."

"That'll be easy at the moment, while this case is on, I won't be home much anyway." He paused. "Sara...I had no idea...I'm so sorry."

"S'Okay." She held him to her. "Let's get back...William will be getting a bit fed up...and we both love him very much...Jeremy, I mean."

Chapter Five

Sunday, 4th August, 10.30 – 18.00 hours
in which the reader learns of George Hennessey's further torment, but also of his delight, and Yellich makes an interesting discovery.

"You are like a dog with a bone." Emily Speake sipped her coffee. "But thanks for this."

"Don't mention it." Hennessey smiled at her. "Sure you don't want anything to eat?"

"Sure. I don't eat much." She glanced sideways out of the café window. High Ousegate baked in the sun, tourists thronged in the street, one or two individuals of varying ages, but the majority were couples or family groups. "I should be out there...day like today, there's money to be made."

"Please don't say that."

"What?"

"Talk about making money...beggars don't 'make' money. People who work, make money."

"Okay," she shrugged. "If you want to get all moral about it...but you did pull me off my pitch. I had made ten quid in just over an hour...sorry...begged ten quid in just over an hour. It was going to be a good day."

"I won't keep you long...weather like this, the tourists will be thick on the ground all day. Anyway, tell me...I have often wondered...how much money do you take off folk in a day?"

"Good days...thirty, forty quid...students are the best, young, with a social conscience...bad day...a few quid. I've never not taken anything. Like I told you, I can make more by begging than by working. It makes no sense to give up begging."

"Well, remember, you can be lifted for it."

"For my own good…yes…you told me."

"So how long have you lived with Leonard Brogan?"

"Few months."

"Where did you live before that?"

"In a hide."

"A what…?"

"A hide. Still go back there…it's in a wood. I like sleeping in woodland…safe as houses. I'm safer in my hide than in one of those high-rise tower blocks with a drunk for a husband. I like sleeping in the wood…weather like this."

"Bit unclean…"

"There's a lake nearby…I wash my clothes and my little body in the lake."

"Yes…Stillwater Lake is a clean lake, you could manage there."

"How did you know it was Stillwater Lake?"

"Leonard Brogan told me. You were there…"

"Oh, yes, yes…I remember."

Hennessey felt a pang of disappointment. That she had difficulty remembering a conversation which had taken place less than twenty-four hours earlier did not bode well for her being a useful source of information. He thought her mentality too badly damaged by drugs or by being in that detached state of mind, which, like drug abuse, prolonged begging can also induce. "So, tell me about Leonard Brogan."

"He's a gentleman. When he found me, I was cold and hungry…the hide is really for summer," again she turned to glance outside, "weather like this. I don't think I would have lasted much longer if Leo's dogs hadn't found me. He took me back to Naseby Hall. I was prepared to do anything he wanted, prepared for the worst he could throw at me, so long as I got warm and had some food...but he did-n't want anything." She shrugged. "Strange guy...before I met Leo, I thought that all men were animals..."

"Had a few bad experiences?"

"One or two."

"Anything we ought to know about?"

"No." Emily Speake shook her head vigorously, in a way which told Hennessey her bad experience was probably very recent and that the police, in fact, ought to know about it. He didn't press the issue.

"So, what did Leo want?"

"He wanted...still wants...to care, that's what Leo wants. He just wants somebody to look after. I got my food...I got my warmth...and I didn't have to give him my body in payment."

"I see. How does he spend his days?"

"Quietly...reading the newspaper...walking in the gar-den...taking the dogs for a walk."

"Friends?"

"Who, me or Leo?" She took another sip of her coffee.

"Leo."

"Must have. I haven't met anybody."

"Family?"

"His son, Luke...think he has a sister – Leo, I mean."

"He has. I saw her photograph."

"Oh, yes."

"Alright, tell me about Luke Brogan."

She shot a worried glance at him, at the mention of his name.

Hennessey paused. He thought the response interest-ing. She remained silent and eventually he felt she should be prompted. "Luke Brogan...tell me about him."

"Don't know him well."

"Tell me what you do know."

"He doesn't come very often. Why did you have to tell Leo that I come into York to beg? He thought I was a good girl...he was really upset with me when you left. He said he felt I had betrayed him, made me promise to stop."

"Yet the very next day, where did I find you?"

"I wanted some money...I would have gone to the Job Centre later in the week."

"Only a minute ago you were anxious to get back out there...to 'make' money."

She looked at the tabletop and swilled the coffee about in her cup. "I'll go later, I promised Leo I would, I can keep that promise...but see, begging...it's like being a smack head..."

"You've been there?"

"Yes...it's much the same sort of thing, it's the way of life...that's the addiction...it's not the heroin for the smack head, it's not the money for the beggar...it's the way of life...it's like a job...no, that's the wrong word, it's what you think you are."

"Your role in life?"

"Yes, it's like that, it's my place to be a beggar."

Hennessey nodded. He could understand that that shift in attitude would be a formidable obstacle to anyone trying to wrest themselves away from an addiction and he thought she was right to make the parallel with drug addicts, begging is addictive...it would fill a beggar's head, they would sit in front of their hat, with a puppy on the end of a piece of string with their sign, 'hungry, homeless, please help' and wouldn't move except to go and eat something. The more alert would ask passing pedestrians to spare a little change, the less alert, the more lost, would be in that strange world of complete detachment. Hennessey began to understand Emily Speake and wondered at her history, he wondered what had brought her to this, at such an early age. He also realised she was delicate...lean too hard and he could drive her back into her psychological bolthole, the hide she had in her head, like the one she had in the woods by Stillwater Lake. If he drove her in there, he would be unable to follow her. "You like Leo," he said softly, "but you don't seem to like Luke...father and son, are they so different?"

She shrugged her shoulders. "Don't really know Luke."

"Well, tell me what you do know of him."

"He's renovating a cottage."

"I know that...tell me about him, his personality."

"He's not like his father."

"In what way?" Gently, Hennessey thought, gently, gently does it.

"He's colder...he's got a side to him I don't like...me and the dogs, we make ourselves scarce when Luke visits."

"The dogs don't like him?"

"No, they keep their distance...they lie down and stare at him."

"That's interesting...ignore a dog's instinct at your peril."

"I'll remember that."

"And ignore your own instinct and intuition also at your peril."

"I'll remember that also." She smiled, briefly, but no matter how brief, Hennessey thought, that smile was most welcome. She was beginning to relax in his company. "Don't know much about him really."

"I see...but what you do know, you don't like?"

"Yeah...if you want...but I don't know much."

"Much?"

"He just gives me the creeps...some men do, some don't...he does. Tell you one thing, Luke Brogan wouldn't give to a beggar. Leonard...Leo would, but Luke, not a chance. Luke would be the kind to steal from a beggar's cup."

Hennessey paused. Emily Speake also fell silent and again looked longingly at the money-laden tourists.

"Do you..." Hennessey broke the silence, "do you know why we visited Leo Brogan?"

"Yes...the body found in the woods by Stillwater Lake. I read the papers and Leo told me."

"Alright...so, do you think we are wasting our time?"

She looked uncomfortable, Hennessey noticed a distinct twitch of her body, an avoidance of eye contact, but she said, "Yes."

"Sure?"

"Sure I'm sure. Leo wouldn't murder anyone. He's just a good, kind old man."

"Not so old probably," Hennessey continued to speak softly, "but good and kind...probably."

"No probably about it. He is good and kind."

"Alright." Hennessey held up his hand. "You're clearly fond of him."

"Yes, and he wouldn't do anyone any harm."

"Okay, I have that impression."

"So why the dog with the bone act?"

"Because of your evasiveness, because Leonard Brogan was similarly evasive and uncomfortable when questioned about Svetlana Zvonoreva, because Naseby Hall holds the key to the murder, otherwise there wouldn't be any evasiveness or discomfort." Hennessey thought, because Naseby Hall has a deep freeze large enough to accommodate the body of a slightly built young woman, because Naseby Hall is a short drive from the woods where the body was found and where the occupant of Naseby hall exercised his dogs', but he said, "Well, it's really our only lead." He then asked, on impulse. "When did you last spend a night in your hide?"

Again there was a clear sign of discomfort, a strong

avoidance of eye contact. Hennessey's heart thumped in his chest as the realisation dawned and before he knew what he was saying, he said, "You know something, don't you?"

"No. No. No." She shook her head vigorously.

"Listen to me, Emily...listen..."

She looked up and held eye contact. He noticed her face had drained of what little colour it had.

"If you saw something, you must tell us, you could be in trouble if you don't."

"Trouble?"

"With the law. This is a murder. Crimes don't come much more serious, any aiding and abetting and you are looking at time in a women's prison, that wouldn't be pleasant for a slightly built young girl like you...you've probably little idea what those powerfully built women can do. You'll become the property of one and when she gets fed up with you, she'll sell you for an ounce of tobacco and you won't get any say in the matter. Not only do you run the risk of losing your liberty, but you will have a particularly hard time in the slammer."

Emily Speake hung her head. Hennessey saw that his words were clearly reaching their mark, having the desired effect.

"You ponder it, Emily...no natural light for 23 hours a day, probably the full 24 in the extreme winter weather when the exercise yard is knee-deep in snow or when the rain is coming down like stair rods...no privacy at all, no personal space...no silence...no solitude...constant banging of cell doors, the screams as yet another fight breaks out among the inmates, and there's you with your love of the woods during a summer's night. All that solitude...all that space...and your freedom even from the restrictions of employment. For you to go to prison, you wouldn't make a good adjustment."

Emily Speake looked at him. He saw fear in her eyes.

"And if you are frightened of someone, if someone has some hold over you, we can protect you. We have a witness protection programme."

"I don't need that."

"So you did see something?"

"I'm saying nothing."

This Hennessey thought, was gold dust, no information at all, but the touching of raw nerves in both Emily Speake and her father figure and protector, Leonard Brogan. It told Hennessey that the police were on the right track, looking in the right area.

"I'm going!" Emily Speake shot to her feet and walked hurriedly out of the café. Hennessey was content to let her go. He enjoyed the comfortable sense of progress having been made. He too stood and left the café. Screwing his panama hat onto his head, he strolled back to Micklegate Bar police station, weaving through the crowd, the buskers, the beggars, whilst making as much use of the shade as he could.

Fifteen minutes later he was sitting at his desk enjoying a cup of tea despite his recent infusion in the café. He relaxed in his chair, leaning back in his shirtsleeves, enjoying the calmer atmosphere of the police station which always seemed to him to prevail on Sundays. His phone warbled. He let it ring twice and then picked it up. "DCI Hennessey."

"Enquiry desk, sir." The voice was youthful, calm, efficient.

"Yes?" Hennessey spoke softly.

"Gentleman here, sir, wishes to talk to an officer in respect of the locket. There was a photograph published in the *Post*, the girl in the wood murder."

"Yes, I know. I'll be there directly."

"It's the same locket, alright." The man was middle-aged, smartly dressed in a light summer suit, cradled his own panama on his lap, which Hennessey noted with a very slight pang of envy was in better condition and of higher quality than his own. The man had given his name as Shawcross, Edward Shawcross, and occupation as jeweller. "I well remember it. Not often we get Russian jewellery, and I mean Russian, not Soviet...that locket was pre 1917, a lovely piece of work."

"Where is it now?"

"Sold it on. I'm afraid we don't have a record of to whom we sold it, all receipts are destroyed after the end of the financial year. Other records we keep for five years as our accountants advise us to, but copies of receipts given to customers, no, we don't. It's really the customers who need to keep the receipt we give when we sell an item, for guarantee purposes in the case of new items and proof of purchase and hence ownership in the case of both new and antique items."

"I see."

"But that locket...caused a lot of interest among the staff."

"Alright. Do you remember who offered it for sale?"

Edwin Shawcross shifted awkwardly in the chair. He glanced up at the opaque skylight near the ceiling of the interview room, then at the heavily stained door and finally at the tabletop. "Well...yes, I do."

Hennessey waited. Shawcross, he thought, was either overacting, or was genuinely finding giving this information difficult.

"Well...yes, I do...this is the reason I have waited."

"Hardly a wait, it was released to the press only a matter of hours ago really. If you had waited until next year then yes, that would have been a delay, and such delays are not unknown...folk wrestle with their conscience, or they suddenly realise the significance of something seen or overheard. Sometimes a deeply buried memory is recovered years after the event itself, so I wouldn't consider this a delay."

"Thank you, that makes me feel better, Mr...?"

"Hennessey."

"Mr Hennessey. Thank you. I have always tried my utmost to be public spirited, but on this occasion I was tormented. I had to talk it over with dear Mrs Shawcross and then this morning, after Holy Communion, I asked our minister for his advice. They both said the same thing...and here I am."

"So, who sold the locket to you?"

"A dear gentleman, and many years we are acquainted with each other, a gentleman in the real sense of the word...a gentleman called Brogan...Mr Leonard Brogan of Naseby Hall, Long Fenton."

Hennessey remained silent. He concealed his excitement at the prospect of the net closing on the gentlemanly Leonard Brogan.

"You are convinced it was Mr Brogan?"

"Yes, you sound as though you know him?"

"We do...we have met each other."

"Then you will perhaps understand my confusion. I was astounded to read the details of that awful murder...at least the details so far as the media have divulged. I am aware that in some cases the police withhold information...but what has been revealed is harrowing. That Russian student...kept in a frozen state for three years, then dumped in a wood where she was found only by chance. I know that stretch of woodland, the trees are quite dense there with heavy shrubbery, you could lose a few bodies in there. I have always said that if the police could sweep the lakes in the Lake District they would close a lot of missing persons files and open a lot of murder enquiries."

"They can't."

"What?"

"Can't trawl the Lakes looking for bodies – just haven't got the resources. All they can do is respond when a team of scuba divers find a body, or it's found by other means, companies testing underwater equipment."

"I see. Well, I was going to say that you might be able to do the same with the woods by Stillwater Lake the vegetation is so dense. I am sure much has been hidden in there over the years."

"Probably has," Hennessey nodded, "and much will continue to be hidden. Human nature doesn't change but, like the Cumbria Police, we can only respond when and if something untoward is reported."

"That is interesting, but I can understand, I know how stretched the police are." Shawcross paused. "You see, I cannot comprehend Mr Brogan being involved in the murder of that Russian girl...not Mr Brogan. I have found him such a warm, such a giving personality."

"How do you know him?"

"Well, I don't know him well, let me make that plain, and if he does have a dark side to him, I would be one of the last to know. I met him at the golf club – we never play together – but we did have a round of drinks at the clubhouse. He wasn't a big drinker nor am I really, still less these days. Heavens, he stopped playing when he fell ill about four years ago."

"He's unwell?"

"Yes...you can tell...even if you haven't seen him before, you must have noticed how pale and slight he is. He pops into the clubhouse from time to time, though not often these days...has an orange juice...never anything alcoholic, except perhaps a brandy or a small measure of whisky...just one..."

"Confess, I did notice that he didn't look to be a fit and healthy man."

"He makes no secret about it. He was diagnosed with cancer four years ago and given five years to live at the very outside...and this is why I agonised over coming to see you. To those who know him, he is a most unlikely suspect...and he is a dying man. If you arrest him today...and if you have grounds to charge him with the murder of that poor young woman, he will be deceased before his case comes to trial...and a man like Leonard Brogan shouldn't die in custody, in a cell, he should be allowed to die at home, the lovely house he created, among the people he loves and who love him...but both Mrs Shawcross and our minister are of the view that I have no ethical right to keep this information from you. They both argue that once I shared my information with them, it put them in a difficult position, ethically speaking, and once I had shared it with them, it was even more incumbent upon me to report it to the police."

"Yes."

"Both also pointed out that Leonard Brogan, dear fellow that he is, may have come across the piece legitimately. I can't remember when he offered it for sale..."

"I was going to ask that question."

"Well, I don't know the answer...more than one year ago...much more...two or three."

"So it could be about the time the girl was reported missing that he came into your shop?"

"Yes, it could." Shawcross sighed. "It very well could. After he was taken ill though, we had a chat about things. Mrs Shawcross had lost her dear sister to cancer and I said what a terrible disease it is, and he said, 'Yes, but aren't we so fortunate that it kills one in three of us'…or one in four, can't remember which…and I said, 'Fortunate? Whatever do you mean 'fortunate'?' And he said, 'Well, isn't it?' and smiled at me – had a very warm smile, still has I presume – and then said, 'Well, if you want to live somewhere where cancer and heart disease are unknown, move to Ethiopia'. He'd spent a lot of his working life in the developing world you see, Mr Hennessey."

"So I understand."

"His point, of course, being that cancer and heart disease are virtually unknown in Ethiopia and many other black African nations because those poor people all die of starvation or genocide before they're old enough to die of cancer. He mentioned an incident some years ago when 80,000 Tutus died in a three-day orgy of violence in Rwanda and it barely merited a mention in the western media. At the time our media was dominated by the question as to whether the Bank of England was going to put up the interest rate by a quarter of a per cent, so he said. His point, of course, being that he has been so fortunate to have had sufficient to eat all his life, and has never been caught up in vast bloodshed which occurs when nations are lawless. Apart from the tragedy of children and young people going down with cancer – that's a tragedy – apart from that, cancer is a disease which speaks of longevity and safe living on the part of the sufferer. That was Leonard Brogan's attitude. He said death held no fear for him, that he considers himself so fortunate to have lived to late middle age in a very troubled period of the world's history and has known nothing but peace and prosperity. He was that sort of man…so…" Shawcross stood. "Well, I don't think I can add anything. So, if you have no questions for me, Mr Hennessey…?"

"I don't think I do. Thank you for coming, Mr Shawcross…appreciate the difficulty you faced. If we want to speak to you again, where can we contact you?"

"Oh..." Shawcross reached into his inside jacket pocket and extracted his wallet. He took a business card from it and handed it to Hennessey. "The shop would be the best place."

"Shawcross and Sons," Hennessey read the card, "Jewellers, Swinegate, York."

"Yes, been there a few years, not for very much longer, methinks."

"Oh?"

"Well the 'Sons' in the title, they were my grandfather and great uncle, the business was started by my great grandfather. I am the last male of the line. I have three beautiful children, all girls, now all married and they and my sons-in-law aren't much interested in the jewellery business. In fact, their interest extended only into obtaining engagement and wedding rings at cost price. So I am the last of the Shawcrosses, of our line anyway. The surname isn't unique, so that will continue, but I will sell the business. I am sixty-three in November. It will sell easily enough, it's a going concern, and sufficient to see me and Mrs Shawcross out."

"If we want to contact you out of business hours?"

Shawcross recited his home telephone number as Hennessey wrote it down. "Mrs Shawcross has a bad heart, so phone-calls and knocking on the door at odd times of the day or night can startle her, could give her a nasty turn. So, if you could avoid the dead of the night, early hours, late hours."

"I'll bear that in mind. Where do you live? Just for our records."

"3, Orchard Way, Hutton Sessay."

"Hutton Sessay?"

"Yes. Why? Do you know it?"

"I live in Easingwold, so know of it...pleasant village."

"Very. And our address lives up to its name...pretty little cottage on a narrow road which leads to an orchard. Well, I'll say goodbye, Mr Hennessey."

Hennessey stood. "Thank you again for coming in. I'll see you to the reception area."

Hennessey bid goodbye to Edwin Shawcross on the steps of Micklegate Bar police station and returned to his office, feeling once again that strange mixture of elation and disappointment. There was the elation that the police were closing down on Brogan, elation that the police were going to look well in the eyes of their Russian counterparts, and an early arrest with strong evidence seemed imminent, yet disappointment that he was likely to arrest a man who seemed saint-like in the eyes of those who knew him. Yet, as he had earlier reminded himself, those thought of and held up as 'good' have revealed a darker side, and equally, those thought of as tyrants and despots have, on occasions, shown themselves to be possessed of a compassion and humanitarianism that none would have thought possible. He sank heavily into his chair and rested his forehead in his palms, his elbows on the desk. He felt a strange heaviness of heart which went beyond disappointment, because for the first time in a long career as a police officer, he seemed to be about to arrest a dying man...and for what purpose? As Edwin Shawcross had just pointed out, Brogan had so little time left and the wheels of justice in England moving, as they do, with such elegant slowness, that Leonard Brogan would most likely be deceased before his case came to court. He would have to take advice. He glanced at the clock on the wall, four p.m., it was his day off. His thoughts turned to home, then returned to the issue of the dying Leonard Brogan who had given his life to developing marginal agriculture in the third world, who offered his home to waifs and strays, who seemed to have a refreshingly philosophical and very unselfish attitude to death, and who was also the prime suspect in the murder of a nineteen-year-old girl, 'cut off', as Hennessey had once read on a gravestone in rural Lincolnshire, 'in the very bud of life'. Time, he thought, to leave it for the day. Brogan wasn't going anywhere and he wanted to consult with the chief superintendent before taking the case even one inch further forward. He stood and reached for his jacket.

Just as Hennessey had done on the day previous, Somerled Yellich found a few moments in which to indulge himself by visiting the grave of Dick Turpin in the cemetery opposite St George's Church. He, too, assumed that, because the headstone was the only vertical one in the bone yard, and the only one still legible, it must have been reconstituted at some point, possibly, he thought, in the nineteenth century for no other reason than that it looked nineteenth century. That was the first impression he had and over the years, he had grown to have faith in his first impressions. They were often, most often, but only most often, right. He allowed himself a brief smile as the old joke came to mind 'Never judge a man until you have walked a mile in his shoes – that way you find out you were right about him all along, and you get to keep the shoes.' He then returned to the gateway of the cemetery, really a gap in the hedge rather than a gateway, where he stood motionless – for he had learned that stillness is a camouflage – and resumed his watch of Fashions, then open for business courtesy of the relaxing of Sunday trading laws. Repeatedly his thoughts turned to Sara and her struggle with Jeremy. He resolved to find ways of spending more time at home. He was about to dismiss his afternoons observations of Walter Tamm's enterprise as 'interesting but ultimately fruitless' when a van turned into

George Street from busy Paragon Street and halted outside Fashions. Yellich watched from his vantage point of approximately fifty yards distant as a male in his thirties slid back the driver's door and stepped nimbly out. As he did so, a young, slender looking woman dressed in a T-shirt and a very low cut pair of denims stepped from the passenger side of the van. The woman strode purposefully into the shop, whilst the man walked to the rear of the vehicle, then turned and seemed to scan the area. What exactly he was looking for, Yellich wasn't sure, but he suspected from his manner that he was checking for any police presence. If the man saw Yellich, it seemed that he dismissed him as a tourist visiting the cemetery, but it further seemed that the man didn't register Yellich's presence at all. Stillness was indeed a form of camouflage. Yellich continued his watch as the man opened the rear doors of the van and revealed a large amount of cardboard boxes.

'Interesting', Yellich said to himself. Trading on a Sunday was one thing, but taking deliveries, very unusual and possibly in contravention of the bylaws. The young woman walked back out of the shop and joined the man at the rear of the van and together they carried the boxes into the shop, one box at a time, the boxes being sufficiently large that they required two people to lift them. The ease by which the boxes were slid from the van and picked up, along with the fact that the woman didn't appear to struggle, gave Yellich the clear impression that the boxes were not particularly heavy. He thought small items of clothing, possibly over packaged in presentation packs. He noted the man; he seemed short but strongly built, and the way he moved spoke of developed muscles, as if a regular attender at the gymnasium. Like the girl, he was casually dressed, though kept the greater part of his flesh concealed. He was dressed in training shoes, jeans, long-sleeved shirt and an

American style baseball cap – blue with a white logo. The young woman clearly rejoiced in her body and her jeans were cut off so severely that the very topmost of her thighs were exposed. Ten boxes in all were unloaded as Yellich watched, the complete cargo of the van. After the last box had been carried into Fashions, the man returned alone to the van to close and secure the doors, then went back into the shop where the woman had clearly remained.

Yellich walked from his vantage point of partial concealment and strolled casually towards the van, reaching for his mobile phone as he did so. As he walked, he casually entered the pre-programmed number for Micklegate Bar Police Station and pressed Send. He identified himself when his call was answered and asked to be put through to the collator. He was by then close enough to read the registration plate of the van which he dictated to the collator. He walked between the van and Fashions taking no obvious interest in either, past the pub and turned into Paragon Street, walking towards Tower Street and Skeldersgate Bridge.

"White Ford Transit, sir?"

"Yes, that's it."

"Registered owner is one Luke Brogan of Ewe Cottage, Long Fenton."

"Really?"

"Yes, sir."

"Alright…see what form, if any, Brogan has…for my attention."

"Very good, sir."

Yellich switched off his mobile and walked to Baile Hill where he joined the walls. The segment of wall between Baile Hill and Micklegate Bar was his favoured stretch, taking the walker through a small area of woodland and offering pleasant green vistas and views of neat rows of ordered terraced housing on the inside of the ancient structure.

'Well, well,' he thought as he passed a family of foreigners, French, he thought, as they struggled with limited English to obtain directions to the Castle from a dog walker. 'Well, well...Luke Brogan delivering goods to Walter Tamm, when Walter Tamm has claimed to have no knowledge of the whereabouts of the said Luke Brogan. Well, well, well...'

Hennessey drove slowly out of basking York, following Bootham, past the Quaker Boarding School and the alleged birthplace of Guy Fawkes, as he followed the canyon of terraced buildings. As Bootham gave way to Clifton, so the buildings became less dense and as Clifton gave way to Shipton Road, there was wide green on his left and suburban development to his right. He drove with the window down, relishing the breeze that was thus created and enjoyed the soothing sound of Radio Four.

A motorcyclist with a female pillion passenger passed him going in the opposite direction. He was driving sensibly, and both he and his pillion passenger were clad in red and grey leathers with black helmets and, thought Hennessey, must be cooking up on a day like today. But they were being sensible and may even be 'Grey Riders'. So called 'Grey Riders' had been given much press coverage of late, often, noticed Hennessey, with a little good humour added to the reportage. Police stopping motorcyclists to speak to them about some minor traffic violation report their shock when upon asking the motorcyclist to remove his helmet, meet not a twenty-year-old but rather a fifty or even sixty-year-old, often with his wife of the same vintage upon the pillion; a professional man enjoying early retirement in the twenty-first century, the age of leisure, all financial pressure off, and so has bought his first motor-bike. They tend to be more cautious than those riders still in or barely out of their adolescence but when in leathers and helmet, look the same.

Seeing the motorcyclist did, as often such similar sights do, cause George Hennessey's brain to switch from a wind-ing down, state of relaxation mode, to focus on the mem-ory of his elder brother, Graham. He wondered what Graham would have done with his life? He would have done something with it, something positive, of that he was certain. The job at the bank wouldn't have lasted, he was just too big for it, it wouldn't have been able to help him. He was already talking about leaving and taking up the study of photography. He had come to realise that photog-raphy is an art form, 'A brush can be used to paint a shed', he would say, 'a chisel can be used to make a rack of shelves, a pen can be used to write a cheque and a camera can be used to take passport photographs, but,' and he would smile as he said this 'but a brush can be used to paint a can-vas, a chisel can be used to carve wood, a pen can be used to write a poem and a camera...a camera in the right hands can be used to create art just as much as a pen or a brush or a chisel'. He had found his vocation, at eighteen; he knew what he wanted to do in life. His parents were a little alarmed because the job in the bank was 'nice and safe', but Graham's mind was set and he was seeking information about entry to art college. George Hennessey was certain that his brother would have become one of the great pho-tographers of his time. Not for him, though, the sleaze of glamour or fashion photography. Graham would have changed the world for the better with hard-hitting right up close and personal black and white images from war zones. While Graham might have alarmed his parents by consider-ing giving up the job in the bank, he had equally delighted them by telling them he was going to sell his bike, his beloved silver and gleaming chrome Triumph on which he used to take young George for a spin on Sundays, down Trafalgar Road to the Cutty Sark and beyond, crossing the Old Father via Tower Bridge and re-crossing on Westminster Bridge and returning to Greenwich. The Triumph had been Graham's passion, but the passion was fading, the motorcycle phase was working out of his system. He was either going to sell the bike to help pay his way through art college where he would study photography as an option, or if he had to remain a little longer at Williams and Glynn's, he would buy a car. That, thought Hennessey, made the tragedy harder to bear. Just a few more weeks and he would have sold the bike. It might also have been easier to bear if he had died doing what he loved, been killed whilst competing in the Isle of Man TT for example, but that dread night, George Hennessey aged about eight, lying abed, listening to Graham kick the Triumph roaring into life and straining his ears as Graham rode away, laying there listening as Graham climbed through the gears, riding down Trafalgar Road until he faded from hearing to be replaced by other more immediate sounds; the boats on the river, the Irishman ambling up Colomb Street, drunkenly chanting his Hail Marys. Then later, the policeman's knock on the door, tap, tap... tap, the hushed but urgent voices, his mother's wailing, his father coming to his room to tell him that Graham had ridden his motorbike to heaven 'To save a place for us'.

Then a few days later, the awful ceremony of the hole and the stone, and the young George Hennessey saw for the first time in his life how incongruous funerals are in summer. Graham's coffin was being lowered as butterflies flitted, as birds sang, as the bells of an ice-cream van, distant yet audible, chimed 'Greensleeves', children were enjoying the summer weather when a tragedy was being played out within the Hennessey family. Weddings should take place in the summer, Hennessey believed, a summer's day can give to a wedding, but good weather somehow detracts from the poignancy of a funeral. Hennessey's father had had the grace to die during the winter months, not a sound was heard as the coffin was conveyed from the church to the grave. And as the priest scattered soil on the coffin and said 'Ashes to ashes...' a sudden, but gentle wind brought a snow flurry, it had seemed so utterly, utterly appropriate. He wondered how he and Graham would have been. He was certain that they would not have drifted apart, and Graham would have been there, always, instead of the awful gap that was in his life which is where his elder brother should have been. Whom would Graham have married? How many children would he have been 'Uncle George' to? Such questions rose in his mind, and upon reaching their zenith, fell, unanswered...unanswerable.

Hennessey drove through Easingwold and upon sighting his house, his heart jumped and he smiled, for sitting on the grass verge outside his house was a silver BMW. It was a car that he recognised well and warmly. He slowed and turned into his driveway as Charles Hennessey appeared at the fence, which served to keep Oscar confined to the back garden during his owner's day long absences. Father and son smiled at each other as Oscar barked and ran excitedly in tight circles at his master's return.

Ten minutes later Charles and George Hennessey sat side by side on wooden outdoor chairs while Oscar lay contentedly in the shade.

"So, where are you next week?" George Hennessey sipped his tea.

"Teeside Crown Court. I am defending a hopeless case, 'I definitely did not cause severe injuries to my girlfriend and the two independent witnesses could not have seen what they said they saw because they were not there'. You get that desperate attitude from twenty year olds who think they can lie their way out of anything, but this...gentle-man...is in his fifties, you'd think he'd know better."

"I told you once," George Hennessey paused to follow the elegant flight of a pair of swans over the house, one just to one side and behind the other, banking together, and keeping perfect station with one another, like two fighter aircraft in formation. "I told you once, chronological age is of no importance in such matters. What is important is the person's emotional development. I confess I have met some twelve-year-olds who are more sensible, more emotionally developed than some fifty-year-olds, though the former tend to be in my personal life, the latter in my professional capacity."

"Yes, I remember you saying that, it helped me to understand a lot...as well as telling me not to waste time arguing with a closed mind. Just lay down the law, and if they don't like it, they don't like it."

"Yes, the cells are full of such people."

"But it's annoying. The weight of evidence against this man is overwhelming. If he'd only plead guilty to it he'd get a much lesser sentence, especially as he's going before Mr Justice Aziz."

"Aziz?"

"Yes...first Asian...first member of any ethnic minority in fact, who's been elected to the Bench. He's developing a very good reputation and he's tipped for the top, but he is known to be harsh with people like my man, who insist on pleading not guilty to hopeless cases and so taking up valu-able court time. Going 'G' with clear contrition, and my man could possibly keep his liberty. He's got a bit of track, but nothing for violence, this is his first. Well, first known act of violence."

"Yes, I like that – first known – that's often the case. The one they get convicted for is the actual umpteenth offence."

"Yes." Charles Hennessey cradled his mug of tea and allowed the sun's rays to warm his face. "But insisting on going NG before Aziz will get him gaol. He won't handle that very easily...despite what he did, he isn't really 'hard man' material."

"Yes...few who are violent towards women and children actually are. The few real hard men I have come across have seemed to pose no threat to women, children, small animals...provided they are allowed lots of space...and speaking of children..."

"They're with their mother and Grandma at a theme park, rather them than me...a theme park on a day like this. It's hot enough for me with all this solitude, this heat among crowds...ugh...but the children wanted to go. I finished the reading I had to do for tomorrow, so I thought I'd drive over, thought you'd be at home."

"Yes...I went in, the body in the woods murder...you'll have read about it."

"Yes, there's a story there. I did wonder if you'd be investigating it."

"Well, yes, there is and yes, I am. Me and Yellich."

"Yes, you've mentioned him before."

"He's a good sergeant to have on your side."

"Strange name..."

"Obscure Eastern European...his Christian name is Gaelic, pronounced *Sorley*, it's spelled S.O.M.E.R.L.E.D."

"Two unusual names – but Charles Hennessey will do me," he smiled, then paused and added, "Couldn't have been easy bringing me up...alone. I mean now I have children, I realise what you did. I have a wife and a mother-in-law from heaven – I couldn't manage if I was alone."

"I wasn't. I had help."

"A succession of women to 'do' for you and Mrs Hunt who watched me when you were at work, hardly the same as a loving partner. You did very well..."

"I didn't want to replace Jennifer and it's a shame you never knew her."

"I feel I have known her, listening to you talk about her...telling me about her."

"Yes...she was...well...a very special person...very special indeed. She's here..." He nodded to the garden. "She's with us now, I can feel her...call me stupid if you like."

"No...I believe you. I wouldn't dismiss such things. I have felt presences before. One of my friends at Cambridge had rooms which he was convinced was haunted by a benevolent spirit. He was lucky."

"Yes, he was. Met someone once who bought a two bedroom flat in an old building which had been converted into half a dozen self-contained flats. When they moved in they were told the flat she had bought for herself and young daughter was always on the market...no one stayed longer than eighteen months."

"Haunted?"

"As you will hear...turned out that the building used to be the cottage hospital."

"Oh no..."

"Yes...and her daughter had troubled, restless sleep from day one...or night one...further turned out that the room which was her daughter's bedroom had been the operating theatre and all the spirits of the folk who had died on the table were tormenting her. She took her daughter into her room, used the haunted room as a store room, and they too were out after a year or so."

"Well, that's what they say...the dead are always with

us...but enough of death...what of life? When am I going to meet your new lady?"

"Soon...she is anxious to meet you. You must come over for a meal, with your family, of course."

"Yes...we'd like that...and I am pleased things are going well for you, you need someone special...you deserve it."

George Hennessey turned and smiled at his son. "Thank you...and you know..." he turned his head and looked out across the garden, "Jennifer approves to, I know she does. I felt her approval...felt that as well."

Chapter Six

Monday, 5th August, 14.30 – 17.10 hours
in which a confession is obtained and George Hennessey helps his senior officer to face his demons.

The three men sat in the room. The silence was broken only by the soft ticking of the clock on the wall and the rumble of traffic which carried in from the junction at Micklegate Bar.

"So..." Chief Superintendent Sharkey leaned back in his chair and pyramided his fingers, holding his hands against his chest, "the finger of suspicion points to Leonard Brogan, no matter how an unlikely murderer he might seem: the name; the location of the house; its proximity to where the body was found; his knowledge of the woods by Stillwater Lake; his evasiveness; his looking uncomfortable at certain points in the interview, and the clincher, the locket, unique and identified by the jeweller who knows Brogan from the golf club...no motive, though."

"None, sir," Hennessey replied. "None yet. There'll be one, I am sure of it."

"Are you?" Sharkey smiled. Quite uncharacteristically, thought Hennessey.

"Yes," Hennessey nodded. "Yes, I am. You see, sir, Brogan does seem an unlikely murderer but he is not the kind of man to kill without a reason, something will have driven him to do it."

"I am inclined to agree, sir," Yellich offered, speaking for the first time since he and Hennessey entered Sharkey's office for the Monday morning 'appraisal' meeting.

"You think the same, Sergeant Yellich?"

"Yes, I do, sir. Brogan isn't impulsive. Petty minded,

emotionally immature, bursting with pent up violence, it's that sort of person who kills without motive. They are the sort that speak of a 'red mist' appearing before their eyes prior to the act of violence. Brogan is a calm, learned man. Strong suspicion is falling on him and it may well be he has done a grand job of concealing the darker side to his nature – but a spontaneous act of murderous violence – I can't see it. Can't see it at all. So, I think DCI Hennessey is correct, there'll be a motive in there somewhere."

"Very well, see what you see. You'll have to bring him in, of course. I hear what you say about him being unwell...so as sensitively... Well, I'll leave that to your good judgement. Now Sergeant..."

"Yes, sir," said Yellich.

"The observations you made yesterday."

"Yes, sir. Well, as DCI Hennessey has indicated, I was observing Walter Tamm of Fashions in accordance with a long running inquiry about fake designer clothing being sold from that outlet."

"Yes..." Sharkey was a man in his mid forties, older than Yellich, younger than Hennessey, immaculately dressed, pencil line moustache. "Yes..."

"Well, as DCI Hennessey has just reported, there existed a tenuous link between Leonard Brogan and Walter Tamm."

"Yes, Brogan's son, Luke...was it Luke?"

"Yes, sir."

"He rented the shop prior to Tamm taking over the tenancy of the shop unit?"

"Yes, sir."

"I see."

"Tamm initially claimed he didn't know of Luke Brogan, then he conceded that he did, but claimed not to have seen him for some time," Yellich continued, "but yesterday, as I was observing, a van arrived outside Fashions, driven by a male with a female passenger. They unloaded the contents of the van, being a number of large cardboard boxes, large but quite light in terms of weight, so it seemed."

"Okay."

"But the number of the van…well, it's registered to Luke Brogan."

Hennessey glanced at Yellich. "Really?"

"Yes, sir, really. So Luke Brogan and Tamm are in contact with each other, despite what Tamm had claimed earlier in the week."

"Interesting…" Sharkey nodded, "that's interesting, and there is a link between the murdered Russian girl, Svetlana…sorry…"

"Zvonoreva," Hennessey prompted.

"Yes…sorry…Russian names…I have always found them difficult."

"I think most westerners do, sir."

"Well," Yellich brought the discussion back on the rails, "yes, Svetlana Zvonoreva was known to have been a client of Luke Brogan when he was running his dating agency…using video tapes…Miss Zvonoreva was keen to remain in the west we understand."

"So there is that link with the Brogan family?"

"Yes, sir…quite a weak link but a link nonetheless."

"As you say, a link nonetheless. What…" Sharkey leaned forwards, resting his elbows on his desk top whilst still keeping his fingers pyramided, "what do we know about the younger Brogan?"

"Quite a different kettle of fish from his father, sir." Yellich opened a manila file he had brought to the meeting. "He's got form, track for handling stolen goods…deception…fraud…"

"Violence?"

"None, sir…looking down the list of previous convictions, what comes over is a slippery, deceitful, sly individual, but not a particularly violent one."

"I see, do we know why father and son are so like chalk and cheese?"

"We believe the Brogan marriage went pear-shaped. They separated and Luke was brought up by his mother."

"Overindulged perhaps?"

"Perhaps. We don't know. Something else we'll probably find out, along with the motive."

"You'll be picking Leonard Brogan up today?"

"Yes, sir. In view of his health, we didn't think a seven a.m. call was appropriate. Let him have a little lunch, then call."

"Good, that allows a little time. Sergeant…"

"Yes, sir."

"I wonder if you'd be kind enough to leave me and DCI Hennessey alone for a moment?"

"Of course, sir." Yellich stood and left the room.

Hennessey settled back in his chair and knew, uncomfortably so, what was coming. He glanced at the wall behind Sharkey, the two photographs were still in place; the one showing a very young Sharkey in the uniform of a junior officer in the British Army, the second, a slightly, very slightly older Sharkey in the uniform of an officer in the Royal Hong Kong Police.

"George, I know I have mentioned this to you before, and I want to imply no dissatisfaction on my part in respect of your performance. You know you enjoy well deserved respect at Micklegate Bar and you get results, good results…but you are approaching retirement."

"I don't want to police a desk, sir," Hennessey protested, and did so knowing he was once again going to hear the story of Johnny Taighe. There was no escape…it was as if Sharkey had to talk about it, it clearly bothered him.

"We had a very able maths teacher at school, George, he left to better himself, took a more senior position with another school, leaving us without a maths teacher in what was our final year, running up to National exams...qualifications."

"Yes, sir."

"There was a shortage of teachers at the time, couldn't recruit anyone of equal calibre to the member of staff who had moved on to better things for himself, so they put a good man in charge of final year maths, Johnny Taighe. I think of him often...good, but ill-equipped. Asking Johnny Taighe to take senior school maths was...well, it was like taking the full cargo from a seagoing container ship and putting it on a trawler, he sank under the weight. And looking back, he was giving out all the danger signals, the false and forced humour of someone under stress: overweight and yet smoking like a chimney, red nose, heavily into the spirits each evening, blotchy complexion. It wasn't healthy. He was a heart attack waiting to happen, and the humiliation he must have felt not knowing what 'interpolation' meant, for example, not being able to solve a problem he'd written on the board and retreating into the class and sitting next to a particularly able boy and asking, 'Where do you think we go from here?' How must that have made him feel? And nobody he could talk it over with, pretending to his colleagues and his family that he was on top of this job, yet knowing he was going to get dreadful results out of that form which he would have to explain because we were thought of as a hardworking form of whom good results were expected."

"Yes, sir."

"Anyway, Johnny Taighe went home one evening, said

he was feeling unwell and keeled over with a massive coronary – stone dead – not able to be revived. He was close to retirement, and just when he should have been allowed to soft pedal those last few months. Well, I learn from that, I wouldn't have had my headmaster's conscience after that and, like I said, I learned from it. It won't happen to any of mine. You are only a few years short yourself, George, you are not telegraphing the same messages that Johnny Taighe was telegraphing in the last weeks of his life. You are not overweight, your complexion is healthy, you don't drink spirits – just beer and then hardly at all – and you don't smoke. You must go home each evening with that comfortable feeling that comes from being on top of things at work but if things are getting too much..."

"I won't hesitate, sir, and I do appreciate your concern."

"Well, so long as you know you can knock on my door anytime."

"Thank you, sir. Will that be all?"

"Not quite, George...if you don't mind."

Hennessey's heart sank. Again, he knew what was coming and again, it was as if the meticulous Sharkey was purging himself of his demons.

"That," he indicated to the photograph of himself in the Royal Hong Kong Police, "that I am not proud of. It's not there to make me feel pride or to impress anybody who sits in front of my desk, it's there to remind myself of my wrong doings...I took bribes."

"You told me before, sir...and as before, I would advise you against broadcasting that."

"I know...but I wasn't there very long. I took little, comparatively speaking. If I didn't co-operate, I'd be found floating among the blue dolphins with my throat slit...and the bribes were to do nothing, to look the other way. It wasn't corruption as we might think of it...tampering with evidence…tipping criminals off…it was more in the manner of, well, the sergeant would tell me not to patrol a certain quarter on a specific night, I wouldn't and there was a packet of readies in my desk drawer the next morning…and also, it was only corruption by Western European standards, it wasn't seen as corruption in China or Hong Kong thinking, that's just the way they worked. But I feel tainted, contaminated. I am worried about corruption in this station, George. My experience in Hong Kong has left me with a deep fear and loathing of it, it just takes one bad apple."

"I am certain no officer here is corrupt, sir…as certain as I can be."

"Alright. But you'll let me know of your slightest concerns?"

Hennessey stood. "Yes sir, of course."

"Thank you, George. Thank you."

Leonard Brogan smiled as he opened the front door of Naseby Hall. He looked down at Hennessey and Yellich from his elevated position at the top of the steps, which led up from the ground to the threshold. "I've been expecting you."

"You've been expecting us?" Hennessey spoke without thinking.

"Yes, Edwin Shawcross phoned me on Saturday evening, he told me he had gone to see you about the locket I sold him, he told me what he had told you. He's an honourable man, a good egg, I like him."

"Confess it does seem a brave and noble thing to have done. I have known few do the same."

"That's the sort of man he is…much better than trying to hide the fact he shopped me…is that the expression?"

"One of similar that would do."

"And such a civilised time as well. I expected it to be a seven a.m. call."

"It usually is, not because we want to be repressive, but it's the most practical time, it's the best time to catch someone at home. But in your case, we made an exception."

"I see...I did always wonder why the police were so fond of seven a.m., now I know. Well, are you going to arrest me?" Brogan paused, even in the midday sun in midsummer could not prevent him looking deathly white. "I'd prefer to do things by the book...keeps us both right."

"Very well, sir." Hennessey strode up the steps and placed his meaty right palm on Brogan's left shoulder; he was alarmed at the skeleton like feel, the man seemed like a bag of bones and he instantly relieved the pressure of his grip. He noticed Brogan smile as if he knew and realised what Hennessey had felt. "Leonard Brogan," Hennessey spoke slowly, clearly, "I am arresting you in connection with the murder of Svetlana Zvonoreva, you do not have to say anything but it may harm your defence if you do not mention, when questioned, something you later rely on in court. Anything you do say may be given in evidence."

"Well, that's a first." Brogan stepped forward, closing the door behind him. Hennessey heard the spring-loaded lock click. "First for me, anyway." He walked beside Hennessey to where Yellich stood beside the unmarked car.

From inside the large house Emily Speake watched Leonard Brogan being gently, but firmly, placed in the rear seat of the police vehicle. She continued to watch as the car was driven away at a sedate speed which, to her, seemed appropriate for the surroundings; the ancient Hall set in the sun drenched and tranquil Vale of York, and appropriate for the age and venerability of the rear seat passenger, which she was pleased to observe, had mercifully been spared the

indignity of handcuffs. She watched the car until it disappeared from sight. Then she rose, wearing only the underwear in which she had slept the previous night and which
she had still not changed out of, she glided – for an observer
would probably describe her walk as a 'glide' – so light and
smooth was her gait – through the cool corridors of Naseby
Hall to where the telephone stood in Leonard Brogan's
study. She consulted the address book kept by the phone
and finding the number she sought, wedged the book open
with a paperweight and dialled.

The red light glowed. The twin cassettes spun slowly and
silently.

"I am Detective Chief Inspector Hennessey, the time is
14.30 hours, the date is the 14th of August. The place is
interview room two at Micklegate Bar Police Station, York.
I will ask the other people present to identify themselves."

"Detective Sergeant Yellich of this police station."

"Leonard Brogan, Naseby Hall, Long Fenton."

"Mr Brogan, would you confirm for the tape that you
have waived your right to have legal representation as
offered by the Police and Criminal Evidence Act?"

"Yes," Brogan nodded, "I have waived said right."

"Alright. Please state your age and occupation."

"Sixty-four, 65 in a few week's time. My occupation:
retired scientist."

"You are going to be asked questions about the murder
of Svetlana Zvonoreva." Hennessey spoke slowly and
clearly. "You are not bound to answer but what you do say
will be taped and may be given in evidence."

"Understood."

"Alright...tell us about the locket, the locket that you
sold to Mr Shawcross. Specifically tell us how you came to

be in possession of it."

"I took it from her after I had killed her."

Hennessey and Yellich glanced at each other. Hennessey felt his jaw drop. The silence in the room was poignant, profound. Hennessey had read of a 'deafening silence', now he understood the contradiction of the phrase. "Mr Brogan, you understand the implication of what you have said?"

"Yes." Brogan hunched forward and he folded his arms in front of him, resting them on the tabletop. "Yes, I do. I feel a great sense of relief now that it's over…I confess I am tired of life, and tired of running from what I have done. I didn't want it to end with this on my conscience. I always, all my life, wanted some notice of my death so I could pick up after myself, leave things as neat as could be. It was a spontaneous act…an act of violence…of aggression but not premeditated. I can at least say that."

Hennessey paused. He was aware of Yellich waiting for him to prosecute the interview, waiting and, he felt, doubtless curious as well as to what approach he was going to adopt in respect of this man who wore his guilt on his sleeve. "I confess, Mr Brogan," he said at length. "I confess I am a trifle concerned at the way…at the eagerness with which you waive your rights. You declined to make the one phone-call you are entitled to make to let someone know you have been arrested, then you decline legal representation. Frankly we don't like that. Despite what you might think, we like to see people in your position exercise all their rights."

"It makes the conviction stronger…safer?"

"Yes. Hennessey held eye contact with Brogan. Despite his confession, he felt a liking for the man, which just would not leave him. "There's nothing more embarrassing for us, for any police force, to have a conviction overturned because we didn't follow procedures. We like all procedures followed…to the letter. So, I invite you again to phone any one you choose and to ask for legal representation."

"Well, again I decline. There is only my sister to phone."

"You have a son."

"Yes, but I am closer to my sister. Luke was really closer to his mother. If I was to phone anybody, it would be my sister. I don't want to alarm her. As for the lawyer…well, I confess. I make a confession…I confess to the murder of Svetlana Zvonoreva. I will sign a statement to that effect. I feel a great sense of peace. I am not running away from what I did any longer."

"Alright, alright. But if at any time during this interview you should want to make a phone-call or have legal representation…"

"I will bear that in mind, thank you."

"So, do you want to tell us what happened?"

"Well…" Brogan shifted his position in the chair. "It began when we were introduced. My son ran a dating agency and he phoned me and said he had found the girl for me."

"Alright."

"Young – very young for one of my years – but she would accept a much older man, she was desperate to remain in the west."

"That girl being Svetlana Zvonoreva?"

"Yes…sorry…she was Svetlana."

"Go on."

"Well, we met, she came to my house and mightily impressed she was. She explained her accommodation in the Soviet Union was very cramped, she couldn't believe I lived in Naseby Hall by myself with the occasional guest. Well, we met again, getting to know each other and the relationship developed. She stayed overnight…and that's when things started to go wrong for us. She was young and lithe and athletic and I wasn't. Wasn't it Shakespeare who wrote about desire outliving performance?"

"Yes. I think he said, 'Is it not strange that desire should so many years outlive performance?'"

"Very good. I am impressed, Mr Hennessey."

"Well even police officers have been known to read."

"I meant no hurt, I apologise."

"So…carry on."

"Well, to use Shakespeare's word, I could not perform."

"I see."

"You understand the importance a man attaches to his virility. As I grew older my sex drive evaporated and along with it, my ability…"

"She must have understood that?"

"She did, but she laughed at me, pointed to me and made derogatory remarks in Russian about me. I couldn't understand what she was saying, not word for word, but I understood the gist of it…that was as clear as day. She had quite an acid tongue…unfeeling…the cruelty of beautiful people is well documented and she was a classic case. She just…wouldn't stop…just didn't let up. Eventually I cracked…she was lying on the floor before I knew what I'd done."

"What had you done?"

"Picked up something and brought it down on her head."

"Picked up what…specifically?"

"A paperweight…a massive paperweight…a rock I picked up from the beach many, many years ago. She turned away from me…laughing…the rock…the paperweight, was beside me on the table. I picked it up and down it came. On the top of her head."

"Go on."

"Well…she was dead…no pulse…nothing at all, so I carried her outside to the outbuildings...laid her in the deep freeze...and there she remained."

"Why wait for three years before removing her?"

"Well, I used a fridge in the house for food. Just me and the occasional houseguest, the occasional guest like Emily Speake. I never had any need to use the deep freeze and kept the outhouse locked. I suppose it was just a question of being out of sight, out of mind. While her body was locked away in a small building on my property, she was in a sense locked away in a small part of my mind...out of my sight and out of my conscience. Then the fridge packed up, it shuddered and died. I needed somewhere to store the food, so I removed her body...took it to the woods by Stillwater Lake and left it in the shrubs, well away from the path...well hidden. I thought it would thaw and rapidly decompose in this heat...but far from that..."

"It was found when still in a frozen state, you and the gentleman who found it must have missed each other by a small amount of time. What time did you leave her corpse there?"

"Early hours – the dead hours...about three or four in the forenoon."

"She was found at about 10.30, I think?" Hennessey turned to Yellich.

"Yes...about that, sir."

"She would hardly have started to thaw...she had been in a deep freeze for about three years, not just dipped in and removed, her very core would have been frozen, the day had only just begun to get significantly warm. She probably would take fully 24 hours to thaw in those conditions...probably longer. So about six hours between me leaving her there and her body being discovered...not such a near miss. Bad luck though. If I had waited for another day...if I had put her a few feet to one side or the other."

"It was indeed a discovery of chance, but it was a discovery and here we are."

"Yes...here we are." Brogan sat back. Hennessey thought he looked relaxed, smug even. Brogan sensed Hennessey's thoughts. "I'm not getting away with it, Mr Hennessey, if that's what you think I am thinking."

"I have no opinion about what you are thinking, Mr Brogan, but I confess you do seem strangely pleased."

"I told you I am pleased it has come to light while I am alive. It is unlikely I will be in this world by this forthcoming Christmas...this will help me die, emotionally speaking. I am pleased, so very pleased that when I unlocked the outbuilding I also unlocked that little space in my mind where I had kept Svetlana's body, and my deed, hidden from my conscience. I feel a sense of relief coming off me...that is why I look pleased, there is nothing strange about it. Really, there isn't...nothing strange at all."

"Very well." Hennessey sensed the interview reaching a natural break, though he also felt that this was far from the end of it all, a very long way from the end. "I assume you are having treatment?"

"Chemotherapy...once per month."

"When is your next appointment?"

"Not for another fortnight." Brogan paused, then asked, "Now what?"

"You will be charged with the murder of Svetlana Zvonoreva, held in our cells tonight. You'll appear before York Bench tomorrow morning, we'll oppose bail."

"I won't request it."

"The magistrates will remand you in custody for seven days. You'll be escorted to prison, probably Full Sutton, but your condition will most likely mean you'll spend your time in the prison hospital, a softer, quieter regime."

"For that, I thank you."

"No thanks needed, Mr Brogan, it's just the way of it."

"You see this is what I meant when I said that I am not getting away with it. I will spend the remainder of my life behind bars. Many prisoners, even many of the so-called 'lifers', can live in the hope that they will breathe free air again. I do not have that luxury. I will find that hard to bear."

"Yes," Hennessey nodded slowly, "for a man of your lifestyle and your life experience...yes."

"I just don't want you to think that I'll be getting away with it. I have also lost my good name and the besmirching of my name will continue after I am dead. That causes me pain...but it's deserved. She was only nineteen after all, and I suppose a nineteen-year-old has the right to laugh at an old man who can't do 'it' anymore."

Yellich drove at a steady pace along the road that stretched over the flat fields of the Vale of York. Hennessey sat beside him, once again fully exploiting the passenger's privilege of being able to glance from side to side. As the journey progressed, neither man spoke. Yellich slowed as he entered Long Fenton and drove sedately through the village. Hennessey noted small shops with bay windows: a post office; a whitewashed cottage with, unusually for the Vale, a thatched roof; a pub called the Green Man and another called The Dexter with a sign outside the door depicting the breed of small cow from which the pub drew its name. Yellich increased the car's speed slightly as he cleared the village and the road once more drove through open fields.

He turned into Naseby Hall and drove up to the front door. He and Hennessey got out of the car, walked up the steps and Hennessey pulled the bell pull. They heard the bells jangling inside the door.

The door was opened rapidly upon the pulling of the bell by a slender woman with shoulder length hair. She was casually dressed in a man's shirt and a pair of white slacks. White and blue coloured sports shoes encased her feet. She wore a wedding band and an engagement ring, the latter with a single rock. Hennessey thought the rock could fairly be described as 'massive'. There was no watch, no other jewellery, just the sign of marriage to a wealthy man. "Yes?" She said in what both cops thought to be a haughty manner, her nose slightly in the air, head to one side, looking down at Hennessey and Yellich.

"Police." Hennessey showed his ID. Likewise Yellich.

"Yes?"

"Can I ask who you are?"

"I am Mrs Teasdale."

"Mrs Teasdale...may I ask your connection with this house?"

"Is that any of your business?"

"Frankly, yes it is." Hennessey allowed an edge to creep into his voice. "This house is a crime scene, the scene of a very serious crime, it is our business who is in this house."

The woman paused. She was clearly intent on answering on her terms. "Very well, I am Mr Brogan's sister."

"I see. May I ask what you are doing here?"

"I think the term is 'house-sitting' and caring for the dogs."

Again Hennessey said, "I see." Then he added, "So you know your brother has been arrested?"

"Yes. Emily, that little girl, phoned me."

"Where is she?"

"I don't know and I don't care...I threw her out."

Hennessey and Yellich felt a pang of dislike for the woman.

"Don't worry about her," Mrs Teasdale continued,

"she'll survive, her kind always do."

"I am afraid I don't share your faith." Hennessey spoke coldly.

"I'm not inviting you to. Well, are you going to stand there or are you coming in? That's what you want to do, isn't it? Enter and search the premises…it is – what did you call it – a crime scene? Come on." She turned and walked into the house. Hennessey and Yellich glanced at each other and followed her.

In the foyer, Mrs Teasdale turned and faced the officers. "So, where do you want to start?"

"We're looking for a paperweight."

"A what?" Mrs Teasdale smirked. On level ground, Hennessey and Yellich were able to asses her height…about 5ft 10" they each thought, and she was in flat soled shoes. They both thought that she would be of aristocratic bearing if 'tarted up' in finery, blending in well at a hunt ball.

"A paperweight."

She raised her eyebrows. "I'd try the study if I were you." She pointed to a room off to the left. "Why? Is that what he killed her with…a paperweight?"

"So you also know why he has been arrested?"

"Yes."

"And you know how he killed her?"

"No…that's supposition…a murder on these premises, then the police come looking for a paperweight. I know that he killed her…I just didn't know how."

"You know he killed her?"

"Yes…he told me." Calm, matter of fact, emotionless, detached.

Hennessey reached for his notebook. "Can we take some details?"

"I thought you were looking for the murder weapon?"

"That can wait…it's not going anywhere."

"Well, come through to the kitchen, I am going to make a pot of tea…I've spent the afternoon weeding his herbaceous borders…I was going to make a pot anyway."

In the kitchen, Mrs Teasdale poured the tea, holding the top on the pot delicately with long fingers. Hennessey and Yellich sat at the table, adjacent to each other, Hennessey on one side, Yellich at the bottom. Mrs Teasdale, having poured the tea and handing a cup each to Hennessey and Yellich, sat opposite Hennessey. "So, ask away," she said, "and make little notes in your little book as you do."

"Oh, I intend to." Hennessey took a ballpoint from his jacket pocket. "So, your name please…your full name."

"Barbara May Elizabeth Teasdale née Brogan."

"Your date of birth?"

"Over 21."

Hennessey glanced at her.

"My husband told me I could say that unless I was a suspect in a crime. He would know, he is a solicitor…Teasdale, Rennison, Blakely and Papworth. My husband is the senior partner. You will not have heard of them, they don't do crime…just civil litigation. My husband says you don't get rich by defending murderers."

Hennessey thought, 'you don't get rich arresting them either', but said nothing and wrote 'over 21' in his notebook. Privately he thought she was late fifties, early sixties, in very good condition for her years, having enjoyed the pampered life of the wife of a solicitor who doesn't do crime because there's no money in it.

"Huge cases…"

"Sorry?"

"My husband takes huge cases…hardly ever make the news, no media interest, defending a company against another if its patent has been infringed, that sort of thing. When both are multinationals, the legal fees run into millions of pounds."

"My son is a barrister," Hennessey sipped his tea, "he only does crime."

"He won't make any money. Not real money."

"Probably not...but I don't think that's his motivation. I think he is motivated by justice being done for the individual."

"Yes...what my husband would call a 'bleeding heart type'."

"Shall we proceed? Your address, please."

"The Manor House, Great Elsworth...two villages in," she inclined her long, slender index finger to her left, "that direction...turn right at the gate, you'll come to Little Elsworth after a couple of miles...quarter of a mile after that is our village. The Manor House is...well...it's pretty unmissable."

"I can imagine. Do you have a telephone number?"

"Of course...landline and mobiles, but I don't have to give you that information either...unless I am a suspect...my husband told me that as well."

Hennessey fixed her with a glare, in response to which Barbara Teasdale held eye contact with him, raised her left eyebrow and remained silent.

"Right...so..." Hennessey pushed the cup of tea away from him. He felt disinclined to partake further of Barbara Teasdale's hospitality. He noticed Yellich do the same, in a gesture of support. "What do you know about the death...the murder of Svetlana Zvonoreva?"

"Only what my brother told me."

"Which was...?"

"Well..." she pursed her lips, "men are such silly, sensitive souls and my brother is no different. She was ribbing him about his inability to perform...just wouldn't let up...instead of throwing her out, he bashed her head in. He just told me it was something heavy that he used...didn't know it was a paperweight. But that's Leo, silly Leo, always digging holes for himself, now he's dug the biggest of them all, but he always was a silly boy. He was my little brother you see, I was always getting him out of scrapes, couldn't look after him in adult life though." She sipped her tea. "You know what he did once? Oh..." Barbara Teasdale shuddered, "such stupidity, had my husband a fit of despair when he found out."

"What?"

"In India...he's been all over the developing world... well, he was working for a company that made pesticides, he was looking at local needs so the company could tailor a product. At the time the Indians in rural areas had a plague of insects that were destroying the crops, Leo made a site visit and do you know what he found?"

"Tell us."

"He found the villagers were capturing the frogs and slicing the legs off to export to France as a delicacy, so he told the Indians to ban the export of frogs legs, let the frog population re-establish itself and they'll deal with the insects...which the Indians did...so the Indian frogs kept their legs...the French 'Frogs' had to look elsewhere for their so-called delicacy and the company lost a contract that could have been worth millions...and silly Leo lost his job. I mean, did you ever hear of anything more stupid? But that's Leo, that's Leo all over...act first and think afterwards."

"But he was right about the frogs?"

"I suppose..."

"So he prevented a developing country spending millions upon millions of rupees on insecticides it didn't need?"

"I suppose...if you look at it that way...but he lost a well paid job and never got near a job that paid as well again."

"Perhaps he thought his act was ethically defensible."

"Oh..." Barbara Teasdale smiled and inclined her head to one side. "You are quite naïve for a police officer, or else you don't yet know my brother sufficiently well. Leo, dear little Leo, wouldn't ponder ethics, nothing so lofty. Leo just didn't know how to keep his mouth shut...like the joke about the men to be executed by Madam le Guillotine...and they chose to face Madame face up as their last act of defiance in life, so the blade severs their throat, rather than the back of the neck. Well, they bring the first guy out and the blade falls and stops an inch from his throat and a great gasp goes up from the crowd, 'Divine intervention' is the cry and he is allowed to walk free...and they bring the second guy out and the same thing happens and he is allowed to walk free, then they bring the third guy out and the same thing happens, except this guy says, 'Ah...I can see your problem, the blade's catching...get me a hammer and chisel and I'll fix it for you." She laughed at her own joke. Hennessey, despite a growing dislike for Barbara Teasdale allowed himself a grunt of appreciation. Yellich did the same. "But you see, Inspector, in that situation Leo would be the third guy...just doesn't know when to keep his mouth shut, just can't stop himself acting...always digging holes for himself."

"I see. When did he tell you this?"

"A few months ago."

"He kept it from you for that length of time?"

"Yes."

"So he can keep his mouth shut then."

Barbara Teasdale flushed with anger. "Perhaps he can...on occasions." She grasped for a reply. "Perhaps he told others, but chose not to tell me."

"Perhaps." Hennessey was not convinced by Barbara Teasdale, he was not convinced at all, it just didn't ring true.

"So…did he tell you why he kept the body for so long?"

"No, he didn't…it was a strange thing to do."

"For one given to impulsive acts, it's not in keeping with his character."

"Probably not."

"Certainly not, I'd say. As a long serving police officer, I can tell you that those who murder impulsively tend to jettison the body as quickly as they can, tends to make our job very easy…those that plan the disposal of the body, by contrast, tend to make our job more difficult."

"But not impossible," Yellich offered.

"Indeed." Hennessey turned to Yellich and then back to Barbara Teasdale, whom he thought was looking less confident, less haughty by the second. "In fact most murders, and I mean much, much more than 51 per cent, are solved… even if we take some time over it on occasions."

"Really?"

"Oh yes, it is true, quite true, that the majority of crimes go unsolved, but that is the majority of all crimes and that is because the police resources are directed to the most serious of crimes…and the majority of those are solved at the expense of lesser crimes…especially the non violent sort."

"Really?" She said again.

"Yes, really…and anybody who involves themselves before or after the crime as an accessory is…well, we tend to wrap everybody up. Something for you to think about. You know, as the wife of a solicitor in a prestigious firm, you should be aware of what you might be getting into."

"I am not getting into anything." She spoke coldly, through gritted teeth.

"Good, I hope so, for your sake. Where do we find Mr Brogan's son, your nephew?"

"What's he got to do with this?" She snapped at Hennessey.

"I don't know, what has he got to do with this? You seem very defensive of him."

"You put me on edge…threatening my husband's position."

"Ah…" Hennessey held up his hand. "I beg to differ, I did not threaten anything. We are investigating a very serious crime here – doesn't get more serious – and it has an international aspect. In all such crimes, the investigating force wants to make a good showing of it and this case is no exception. So, where is Luke Brogan to be found? We are just backtracking the investigation, we'd like to hear from Luke about introducing Svetlana to his father."

"I don't see…"

"You don't have to see, Mrs Teasdale. We do. We have to see." Hennessey leaned forward. "Where is he to be found?"

"Well, all I can tell you is his address…on the other side of the village. Ewe Cottage. I haven't been there, but I gather you can ask at the post office or at the Green Man."

"Thank you. Now, if we could look at the study…hoping to find a likely looking murder weapon in the form of a paperweight."

Driving back to York, a paperweight in a sealed production bag on the rear seat, Hennessey said, "Sleep on it."

"Sir?" Yellich kept his eyes on the road, the traffic leaving York was increasing in volume, the rush hour was commencing.

"What we have been told this afternoon by Leo Brogan and the icy Mrs Teasdale. Sleep on it. Tomorrow we will debate it."

"It's full of holes, sir…"

"I know. I know. Which is why I want us to sleep on it."

"Very good, sir."

It was Monday, 17.10 hours.

Chapter Seven

Tuesday, 6th August, 09.00 – 15.30 hours
in which Hennessey and Yellich return to Long Fenton, and a second confession is made.

Hennessey and Yellich sat in their shirtsleeves in Hennessey's office, sipping hot tea.

"Too easy."

Yellich nodded.

"The whole thing just doesn't ring true."

"Brogan eager to confess to clear his conscience..." Yellich swilled the tea that remained around his mug. "A man like him murdering someone in the first place. He's given his life to agriculture in the developing world...he takes waifs off the street and doesn't exploit them. Would a man like that get involved with a nineteen-year-old girl? I can quite understand that a Russian female desperate to remain in the West would countenance marriage to a much older man – but would a man like Brogan accommodate her?"

"I don't think he would."

"Neither do I, sir. Neither do I. Especially since he knew he was ill."

"Yes...good point," Hennessey nodded. "Good point."

"Didn't believe his sister either," Yellich added. "I didn't believe her on two levels."

"Neither did I...on two levels...but go on."

"Well, in the first place, Leonard Brogan seems a pleasant, warm character who may or may not have a dark streak...he may still be telling the truth."

"Indeed," again Hennessey nodded. "We mustn't close our minds to that possibility, never ignore the obvious."

"But his sister…acid mouthed…stuck-up cow. I find it hard to believe that they could be so different in terms of personality and be brother and sister. They must have had the same upbringing – even if they pursued different lifestyles – and her attitude was far from sisterly, running her brother down like that. It was as if she was feeding him to us."

"Yes, that was impossible to ignore as was her cynical interpretation of the story about the frogs. That can equally be interpreted as being the noble act of a gentleman who realised that the company he was working for had wilfully abandoned the moral high ground in order to exploit the Indian Government. Just let the frog population re-establish itself and you won't need insecticides…it's devastating in its simplicity and as I said, noble in its reason. Not the attitude of mind of a man who would kill because a female student laughed at him."

"Allegedly."

"Yes, Yellich, you're right…allegedly. I have known impulsive and emotionally immature men kill for that reason, but as we seem to be agreed, Leonard Brogan is not emotionally immature, nor does he strike me as impulsive. What's happening here, Yellich?"

"Confuses me as well, skipper. But whatever it is that's going on, it's…well, it's solemn, solemn indeed."

Hennessey stood. "Grab your jacket, time we met Brogan the Younger."

Hennessey and Yellich drove out to Long Fenton, to the Green Man. The main door of the building was open and Hennessey and Yellich walked into the lounge bar where a middle-aged woman was vacuuming the carpets, having evidently put all the chairs on the tables and the bench which hugged the wall of the room. The roof beams were low and of real wood, the bar was small, circular and unobtrusively placed in the corner of the room, a glass cage hanging on the wall contained a stuffed badger. Prints depicting hunting scenes decorated the remainder of the walls.

"We are not open yet, gentlemen." The middle-aged woman stopped vacuuming but didn't switch the machine off. There was a note of alarm in her voice.

"I should hope not." Hennessey smiled and showed his ID. "Police."

"Oh…I hope there's no trouble. Do you want to see my husband…he's the landlord?"

"No, there's no trouble, we were told to ask at the pub for Ewe Cottage."

"Oh…" the woman groaned. The name clearly had some significance for her and evidently not a pleasant significance. She switched off the vacuum cleaner by means of pressing a button with her foot and wiped her hands on the green smock which covered her jeans and T-shirt. "Glad he's going."

"Who?"

"The young man who bought it." She walked towards the offices.

"Who is that?"

"Young man called Brogan, Luke Brogan, just a bad lot, just causes trouble…is always looking for a fight, drinks in here, well, has to, no other pub in the village will serve him. Never been badly enough behaved for my husband to ban him, but he's been close on a few occasions."

"Really?"

"Yes, really." The landlady swept past Hennessey and Yellich, as if eager to direct them, as if she thought the police calling on Luke Brogan was no bad thing, no bad thing at all. "This way."

"Wait a moment, please."

The woman stopped and turned. "Yes?"

"What do you know about Luke Brogan?"

"Enough to know I don't like him. "

"What does he do for a living?"

"Now you're asking...no visible means of support...is that the phrase? Tries to sell things in here, watches, that sort of thing. Nobody wanted to buy anything from him, had that smell of proceeds of a burglary about them. My husband challenged him, he wouldn't say where they came from, so my husband told him to stop selling them...never did that again. Problem is, he's a village lad, he grew up here."

"Really?"

"Again, as I said a minute ago, yes, really. His father has a large house in Long Fenton. Luke grew up with his mother in a house at the other edge of this village...she died recently, well, a few years ago now."

"So we understand."

"Not very old...just my age now, fifty-two." The landlady shuddered, "Makes you think...makes you value your life. I've never lost anyone close to me." She reached out and touched a highly polished arm at the end of the line of the bench. "Both parents still alive...husband...three children...even Mr Tibbs is still with us."

"Mr Tibbs?"

"Our black cat...we had him before we had the children, he's pushing thirty now. I know I have been lucky like that and I appreciate it, but going at fifty-two...of natural causes...that's badly short-changed."

"What was she like?"

"Mrs Brogan? She was a weak-willed creature, nervous, whimpery...shuffled as she walked as if permanently apologising for her presence...smoked heavily, in a nerve calming way. She came in here a few times when it was quiet, bought a gin and lit up. You could almost see the tension leave her as she took the first drag of nicotine...never smoked in the street, never that desperate, but they said that the ceiling of her living room was yellow with nicotine stains and the kitchen and bedroom ceilings were not a deal better."

"You saw Luke grow up then? I mean, watched him grow from a distance?" Hennessey asked.

"Yes. He's older than my children, so they escaped his influence. He was uncontrollable...a bit wild...a lot of vandalism in the village was down to him when he was about fourteen or fifteen, but nothing could be proved, he was too foxy, he knew all the pathways in and around the village. He'd pan some fella's greenhouse glass, dart into the woods, come out by a gennal, dash across the high street, up another gennal, out into the fields and be in the youth club at the far end of the village playing harmless games...coming over all innocent...while folk were looking for the culprit near the greenhouse, or whatever. Fortunately there isn't a railway line near here because if there was, Luke Brogan was just the type of vandal to derail a train and think it was a huge joke. It's what comes of growing up with a father whose absences are both long and frequent and with a weak willed, timid mother as your only parent."

"Seems so."

"Well, he avoided getting into trouble with the police – you chaps – just wasn't caught, but made an impression in the village among the lads and lassies of his age group...he was top dog for a while. Then the village couldn't hold him and he went to live in London and that taught him about himself...didn't it just."

"What do you mean?"

"Well, he was back within a few weeks. He left in May

as I recall and was back by July. I overheard him in here one night talking to the other lads, I'll never forget what he said, he said, 'Nobody knew who I was, they didn't get out of my way in the street...and in pubs I had to wait to be served', and so he came back to Long Fenton where everybody knows who he is, where they get out of his way when he walks down the high street and where we serve him the instant he comes into the pub, not because we like it that way, but because the other customers stand aside and let him get to the bar and withhold their orders until Luke Brogan is served," she paused, "and that's probably why my husband has been loath to refuse to serve him...a rural community...if anything happens, the police take an age to get here, not a great deal of help to us when all our windows get put through at 3.00 a.m. – and probably followed by a petrol bomb – so, yes, I suppose you can say we are intimidated by him."

"Well that's given us a good measure of the man, thanks, Mrs...?"

"Scanlon."

"Scanlon. Thank you, Mrs Scanlon. Do you know why he's leaving Ewe Cottage?"

"He can't make the payments."

Hennessey and Yellich had followed Moira Scanlon's directions and had walked the short distance to Ewe Cottage, 'Left after the butcher's, down a path, Ewe Cottage is white painted, on the right, has the name on the gate'. Hennessey and Yellich pushed open the gate and as they did so, saw a man in a lightweight summer suit standing in the living room of the cottage.

"Well, someone's at home." Hennessey led the way to the front door.

"Evidently," Yellich murmured, "but if that's Brogan the younger, he wasn't the bloke who was delivering packages to Tamm's shop on Sunday."

"We'll soon see." Hennessey extended his hand as he reached the door and pressed the bell which sounded the Westminster chimes. He thought it not very 'cottagey'. His preference would have been for a simple brass knocker, or a bell hanging on the wall by the door to be rung like a ship's bell by any visitor.

The door was opened by the man wearing the light-weight suit. "Yes?" he asked, cautiously, defensively.

"Police." Hennessey showed his ID

"Oh, yes." The man visibly relaxed. He was clean-shaven, ginger hair, he held a clipboard in his hand.

"Who are you...if you don't mind telling us?"

"Walter Bestie, of the Harrogate York and Ripon Building Society. I'm making a site inspection."

"We were looking for Luke Brogan."

"He used to live here." Bestie scratched his forehead with his clipboard.

"Why did he leave?" Hennessey thought Bestie to be about thirty years old. It was then that Bestie also told the officers that Brogan couldn't make the monthly repayments. "So we had to repossess. Not a pleasant thing to do...it's either unpleasant or very unpleasant. In this case it was only unpleasant. "

"What's the difference?"

"Depends who and why they are being evicted: a family who can't make the repayments because of no fault of their own; ill health; accident; redundancy on the part of the breadwinner – that's very unpleasant. Single man like Brogan esquire who can't make payments because his business ventures keep failing, well...that's only unpleasant. So I am here making a site inspection, it's about the only job I get to do that gets me out of the office. I tell you, an office is no place to be on a day like this, even if it is air-conditioned."

"Do you mind if we take a look round?"

"Be my guest. He's moved all his personal possessions out, as you'll see."

Bestie stepped aside and the officers entered Ewe Cottage. 'Most of his possessions' was clearly an understatement, the cottage appeared to have been stripped bare, down to the floorboards, only fixtures and fittings remained.

"He left the wallpaper though," Bestie offered the cheery observation. "So he's not really a dyed in the wool Yorkshireman, otherwise that would have been scraped off and sold to a paper recycling business...but then I come from Lancashire so I'm allowed to be a little prejudiced."

"Well, I'm a Londoner," Hennessey enjoyed Bestie's humour, "so I am comfortably neutral."

"But I'm a Yorkshireman and am not amused," Yellich said, but said it with obvious levity.

"Well," Bestie looked round, "it's hardly a stately home, so you don't need the guided tour. I've got the inspection to complete..."

"How much land is there attached to the cottage?"

"Well, the front as you have seen...a little at either side...a fairly generous garden at the rear going down to a pond, quite a nice feature in my view, a pond in a garden has a relaxing quality...I always find anyway."

Hennessey said that he knew what Bestie meant, but didn't elaborate.

"It's all clearly defined by a hawthorn hedge...two outbuildings...oh, he left his deep freeze as well...so definitely not a very Yorkshire Yorkshireman."

"Where's that?" Hennessey failed to disguise the surprise he felt. "The deep freezer."

"In one of the outbuildings...the first you come to...the second contains kindling."

The deep freeze was as Bestie had said, in the nearest and largest of the two outbuildings. It was similar to that in Leonard Brogan's home, of industrial size, the sort used in hotels and hospitals and, as both officers thought, quite long enough to accommodate the body of a short, slightly built person...it had been defrosted and cleaned.

"Better get the scenes of crime officers out here," Hennessey spoke slowly, "doubt if we'll find anything. In fact I am certain they won't, but we'd better do it...procedure being procedure."

"Very good, boss." Yellich reached for his mobile phone.

Hennessey walked back inside Ewe Cottage and located the jovial Bestie in an upstairs room. "Where is Brogan now? Do you know?"

"Not personally...the Society would contact him via his solicitor or direct if he gave us a forwarding address. I could phone them..." He too reached into his jacket pocket and extracted a mobile phone.

"Thanks."

"Yes..." Bestie switched off his phone, "all contact is via his solicitors, Ellis, Burden, Woodland and Lake."

"Yes, I've heard of them. They do a lot of criminal work. I know their offices...now I'll have to ask you to leave the premises."

"To leave? I only just got here."

"Good...not touched a great deal then?"

"Hardly anything. Why?"

"Well, the cottage and grounds are possibly a crime scene, possibly...but I am taking possession of it for the police."

* * *

Hennessey showed his ID to the young man, grey suit, red tie, who snapped to attention as soon as Hennessey and Yellich entered the premises of Ellis, Burden, Woodland and Lake on Coppergate and who introduced himself as 'Mr Cooper', adding, 'How may I help you, gentlemen?'

"We want to contact a client of yours – of the firm – don't know if this is the correct address. We know you are a huge firm with many offices."

"Indeed, yes, sir."

"Well, the person we want to contact is a gentleman called Brogan, Luke Brogan, late of Ewe Cottage, Long Fenton."

Cooper leant forward and tapped Brogan's name into a computer keyboard, eyeing the monitor as he did so. Twenty-first century technology amid an eighteenth century building of low beams, narrow staircases and a sloping floor, yet so used were they to computers, that the machine didn't seem out of place. "Here we are...Luke Leonard Brogan...Ewe Cottage."

"Sorry?" Hennessey glanced at Yellich, who raised his eyebrows. He turned again to Cooper. "Did you say Leonard?"

"Yes..." Cooper read the monitor. "Yes...here it is, as clear as day...Luke Leonard Brogan."

"A patronym!" Hennessey gasped. "So both Brogans... Brogan the elder and Brogan the younger are both Leonard..."

"Both possibly known as Leo." Yellich added. "Well, knock me down with a feather."

"He is a client of Mr Watson of our Bootham branch, but all the details seem to be here."

"His address...?"

"We have a forwarding address...care of Tamm, he's out in the sticks too, Kings Wichling...it's on the way to

Driffield...number one, The Lane, Kings Wichling."

"Thanks," Hennessey said as Yellich scribbled the address in his notebook. "Thanks, very much."

Walking down Coppergate which baked in what the media had announced to be 'record temperatures' and were reporting the bookmakers bracing themselves for massive payouts should the mercury reach 100°F for the first time in Britain since records began, sliding between sweating tourists, Yellich asked, "What now, boss?"

"Indirect approach, I think, Yellich." Hennessey mopped his brow with a folded up handkerchief. "The indirect approach. Do you have enough evidence for a warrant to search the premises of Fashion?"

"I think so...his track record...suspicious deliveries observed on a Sunday, which is contrary to the by laws of the City of York..."

"Well, let's obtain one. I think we should nudge Mr Tamm, see how he flutters."

The twin cassettes of the tape recorder spun slowly, silently. The red recording light glowed.

"The time..." Hennessey glanced at his watch and double-checked with the clock on the wall, "13.10 hours." He noticed both Tamm and the duty solicitor check the time with their own watches. "The date is Tuesday, 6th of August. The place is interview room one of Micklegate Bar Police Station, in the City of York. I am Detective Chief Inspector Hennessey. I am now going to ask the other people present to identify themselves."

"Detective Sergeant Yellich."

"Fiona McGuire, of McGuire and Golightly, duty solicitors, engaged by the police under the terms of the Police and Criminal Evidence Act."

"Walter Tamm." He was dressed in a smart lightweight suit.

"Thank you, Mr Tamm." Hennessey thought Tamm looked resigned.

Hennessey paused. "Mr Tamm, you have been properly cautioned, you know you are not obliged to say anything..."

"I understand." He spoke with a gently quivering voice.

"There are two things we want to talk to you about."

"Two?" Tamm, clearly alarmed, glanced at Miss McGuire who was severely dressed in a black pinstripe suit, laden with rocks and jewellery but devoid of an engagement or wedding band. Clearly to all who met her a 'Miss', but young and attractive, a woman who could pick and choose, and who clearly knew she could pick and choose, so might an observer conclude. "I thought it was just the dodgy gear?"

"So it is bent?"

"No...it's not bent, it's not stolen...it's imitation."

"That's a crime, selling designer clothes as being the real thing when they are nothing of the sort."

"I know."

"Mr Tamm..." Miss McGuire turned to him.

"No...it's alright, they've got me bang to rights...my old man was a blagger."

Miss McGuire glanced at Hennessey. Dark hair tied in a ponytail.

"A career criminal," Hennessey explained.

"Ah..." She nodded her thanks. Her pen remained poised over her notebook.

"He told me...if the cops get you bang to rights, all you can do is put your hand up, any struggling just makes it worse...he said it's like falling in quicksand...he said the theory of surviving quicksand is to stay still...your body will float...people get sucked into quicksand because they panic and start struggling and squirming about...that just works you deeper into it."

"Not a theory I'd like to put to the test," Hennessey smiled. "But I understand the parallel your father draws between quicksand and the law. It's good advice and you have done well to heed it."

"Nothing else I could do, you've got your warrant, your blokes are emptying my shop...they'll find the stuff we unloaded on Sunday, all cheap, tacky stuff with fancy labels. I knew you were closing in on me when you called. I should have listened to my instincts and let things cool off. I had dodgy stock in the back but not much...but you seemed more interested in Brogan, so I took a chance."

"Why did you tell us you didn't know Luke Brogan?" Hennessey paused. "And before you answer that, I have to say that the letting agency told us that you knew each other personally...they just mentioned it in passing but it chimed with us because just an hour earlier you denied point blank that you knew him. Similarly, the reason we obtained the warrant to search your premises was because we observed the shipment being delivered."

"Taken from a transit van registered to Luke Brogan," Yellich added.

"You've been watching me?"

"You have been under loose surveillance for a while, not 24/7 but if passing we would cast a curious glance in your direction. I was paying my respects to Dick Turpin on Sunday...saw the delivery go down."

Tamm glanced sideways at the floor. "I can't do gaol time, I wouldn't survive...not with those apes in there."

Hennessey pondered that the finely made Tamm, the whimpering Tamm, would indeed find life on the inside somewhat...challenging. "Yes...it's not an easy ride."

"So, I help myself. I admit what you can prove."

"Good," Hennessey smiled. "We've got off to a good start. Now tell us what you know about the murder of Svetlana Zvonoreva, the Russian student."

Colour drained from Tamm's face. His eyes widened. His jaw dropped. Hennessey thought, thank you very much, Mr Tamm, that's another good start. He observed. "You seem to know her?"

"Do I?"

"Do you?"

"What?"

"Know her?"

"No…I meant you thought I seemed to know her. I wondered why you said that?"

Hennessey saw no reason not to tell the truth. "Because, Mr Tamm, at the mention of her name your eyes dilated, because your jaw dropped and because colour drained from your face. So how about a little truth from you?"

"We are often in this position." Yellich added. "We 'read' people, we are trained to do it…we 'read' rooms, houses, streets…and we say to you as we have often said in this and other interview rooms, you can work against yourself, or you can work for yourself."

"You are wriggling, Mr Tamm, struggling…remember what your father said about quicksand."

"That's only if I'm bang to rights…don't struggle if you're caught bang to rights. I'm only bang to rights over the gear in the shop…okay, it's not kosher."

"Where did you obtain it?"

Tamm gave Hennessey a pained look as if to say, 'You should know better than to ask that question'.

Hennessey let it go. It was Yellich's case, not his, and a minor investigation beside the investigation into the murder of Svetlana Zvonoreva. "So…you know something about the murder of Svetlana Zvonoreva? The question is

what? And the other question is, why are you frightened...or who are you frightened of? Brogan? That is the
younger Brogan, Luke, also called Leo."

Tamm made no reply. He looked nervous as he glanced
about him. Fiona McGuire sat motionless, but alert, king-
fisher-like, poised as if about to strike at our pounce upon
anything that was in breach of PACE.

"Svetlana wasn't involved with Leonard Brogan, was
she? She was involved with Luke. It was Luke who was the
Leo in question and it wasn't the deep freeze at Naseby
Hall that was Svetlana's resting place for the last three years
was it, it was the deep freeze at Ewe Cottage, wasn't it?"

"Was it?"

There was a lull in the conversation, a tension developed
in the room. Hennessey was content to let the tension eat
away at Walter Tamm. Eventually Hennessey spoke. "You
know, Walter, flogging dodgy gear isn't such a bad crime as
crimes go. Some people even think it's a so called 'victimless' crime, though of course there is no such thing. They're
happy...you, the retailer, make a tidy profit, so does the
supplier, nobody's life is being destroyed as with heroin or
cocaine...nobody's had violence done to them, and
nobody's lost their life...'victimless'."

Tamm glanced at Hennessey, he looked puzzled.
Hennessey read him and said, "Where I am going with this,
Walter, is that knocking out dodgy gear is one thing...mur-
der is another...even conspiracy to murder is serious. For
the dodgy gear you might even escape the slammer. For
murder...even conspiracy to murder, you eat porridge for a
long time."

"You don't look like the sort of bloke that would survive
prison," Yellich observed, "not really a man's man are you,
more of a ladies' man. Your shop selling very small items of
female clothing...men like you don't do too well in the

armed services or prison...not really into male bonding are you? Men don't like you and you don't like men."

"What are you saying to my client?" Fiona McGuire asked quietly without looking at either Hennessey or Yellich. "It is close to coercion."

"Just advising Mr Tamm that as Sergeant Yellich has just said, he can work against himself or he can work for himself. Prison is a real possibility here, Miss McGuire, you know that and we want Mr Tamm to know that."

Walter Tamm drew a deep breath. "I don't know anything about the murder of the Russian girl."

"You must now charge my client in respect of the murder of the Russian lady or release him." Fiona McGuire spoke with quiet authority.

"Alright." Hennessey sat back in his chair. "We will be charging you under the Sales of Goods Act," he paused, "but as for Ms Zvonoreva, we'll see what we find, Mr Tamm...but please be advised, if you know something about that murder...especially if you didn't do it...and we find out the extent of your involvement, well then...then it will be too late to help yourself."

Unexpectedly Fiona McGuire turned to Walter Tamm and said, "The officer is right...that's good advice, it's as good as your father's advice to you." Then she turned to George Hennessey and said, "You're not detaining my client under the Sales of Goods Act, surely?"

"No...he'll be charged and released pending trial."

"Very well." She turned again to Tamm. "I'll have a chat to you outside about this, as you have been told, working for yourself or working against yourself."

Yellich escorted Fiona McGuire and Walter Tamm to the exit of Micklegate Bar Police Station and then walked to the

CID corridor and thence to Hennessey's office.

"Never known a solicitor to talk like that before." Hennessey picked up the kettle and tested its weight. Finding sufficient water therein he added, "Coffee?"

"Tea, please, skipper." Yellich sat relaxed and uninvited in the chair in front of Hennessey's desk.

"Tea, it is."

"Yes, as you say…if such advice is given, it's often not in our hearing."

"But it was good advice."

"Do you intend to pick Brogan up?"

"Yes…oh yes…let Tamm contact him for us, let him work out a nice complicated alibi that will crumble under pressure." He handed Yellich a mug of tea.

"We can arrest him in connection with the imitation clothing, it's a useful lever."

"Yes," Hennessey sat at his desk, "yes, indeed…all help gratefully received. You could make a start by phoning his solicitors. What were they called?"

"Ellis, Burden, Woodland and Lake."

"Of course," Hennessey smiled, "should have remembered. In fact, they give my son a lot of his work…rather, the chambers my son belongs to. Anyway, obtain Luke Brogan's address."

"Right, boss."

The phone on Hennessey's desk rang. He let it ring twice, as he often did, before answering it. Yellich heard him say, "DCI Hennessey…really? Alright, I'll be down directly." Then he replaced the receiver and looked at Yellich. "Well, well, well…"

"What is it, boss?"

"Little Miss Speake."

"She of the pavement and she of Naseby Hall?"

"The very same…"

"Is at the enquiry desk, wishing to talk to me or anyone involved with the murder of the Russian student."

"She said 'murder'?"

"Apparently."

"Well, well, well," Yellich echoed. "Well, well, well, indeed."

"She's come to give information so I'll chat to her myself...no need to make it a two hander."

"Okay." Yellich stood. "I'll make that phone-call."

"I was in my hide, they never saw me, but I saw them. It was almost light and I have developed good night vision anyway. I recognised the van...I could see it through the trees."

"They?"

"Brogan and Tamm." Emily Speake fidgeted nervously in the seat. "You're not taping this?"

"No." Hennessey smiled. He tried to relax her. "No, you are giving information. We'll see what you say and, if appropriate, we'll put it down in the form of a statement."

"Okay."

"So, which Brogan are we talking about?"

"Luke, the son."

Hennessey nodded.

"He's got some hold over Tamm, don't know what, but Tamm's a minor player."

"Why are you telling me this?"

"To save Leo."

"Save him?"

"I saw you arrest Leo...I phoned his sister and she came over to the Hall because I told her that I knew it was Luke who had dumped the body. If I hadn't said that, she probably wouldn't have come over, but she came over and told me what had happened."

"What did she say?"

"Well, Luke tried to start a dating agency..."

"Yes..."

"The Russian girl was a customer...a client."

"Yes...this we know."

"Well, Luke became besotted with her...she didn't want anything to do with him. Luke's...I don't like him...he's a nasty piece of work...he whacked her over the head...Tamm was there..."

"Where did this happen?"

"At the premises of the agency...it's now Tamm's trendy clothing shop."

"We know...we know that as well."

"They put her in the car they had and drove her to Luke's cottage...and...they put her in the deep freeze." Emily Speake seemed to Hennessey to be fighting back tears. "He kept her there all this time...like a possession."

"Do you know whether she was conscious or unconscious or even alive when they put her in the freezer?"

"I don't...only Tamm or Luke Brogan can tell you that."

"Alright...and how do you know all this?"

"Leo's sister told me. She said that soon after the murder, Luke confessed to Leo, his father, he was scared, he had to tell someone. She said that Leo blames himself a lot for the way Luke has turned out...spending his life in the developing world...at the expense of being a father to his son. Me, I think Luke was just born bad...he's just not a Brogan...anyway, then Leo knew he was ill so he took a locket to a jeweller he knew...the locket belonged to the girl."

"He laid a false trail?"

"Yes, that's what Leo's sister said... Right or wrong it was Leo's way of making up to his son, the last thing he could do with his life was to give his son a second chance'."

Hennessey nodded, but remained silent. Now, he thought, now Leonard Brogan's confession which seemed so full of holes...now it makes sense.

"So...Leo's sister wanted me to keep quiet about seeing the body being dumped and she told me why...'Keep quiet for Leo's sake,' she said, 'he's a dying man...only a few months left...this is the way he wants it'."

"Why did they move the body, because the cottage was being repossessed?"

"Yes...I believe so."

"And why did you choose to come forward? You seem to feel a debt to Leonard Brogan, yet you are going against his wishes?"

"Yes...I owe him...I owe him more than you can know. He's been like a father to me...a good father...I won't have his name blackened. I won't have a...a...thing like his son getting away with murder. I also thought about waiting until after the funeral so at least he would die thinking he had done right by his son...but Leo...you've seen his house, the garden...the entire planet has been his world...a man like that can't be allowed to spend the last few months of his life in prison...especially when he is innocent...innocent of murder anyway."

"Yes..." Hennessey spoke softly, "laying a false trail was an offence, though in the circumstances, we won't prosecute...little point."

"Little point...and if I did delay telling you what happened, it would be keeping something from Leonard I had no right to keep from him. No matter what he thought. It's what he told me...long chats in front of a log fire in the hall on winter evenings...the importance of being open in relationships...how to conduct your life. That's what he was like, you see...he didn't just take me off the street, he took me off the street and gave to me, emotionally speaking, like a parent. He might hate me for doing this, but I am pleased I have done it."

"So am I, Emily. So am I." Hennessey stood. "I'll go and get some statement forms, then we'll write your statement...get you to sign it."

"What will happen to Leo?"

"Well, we'll interview Walter Tamm. If he's sensible the charges will be dropped against Leo and he'll be discharged from custody...possibly even today"

"Good. I think I've done the right thing. He once said, 'We have such hopes and fears for our children and we never know if what we are doing is right'. It's one of the last things he said to me. I thought it strange because he'd always seemed so certain...I mean like a wise man is certain, not like pigheaded people are always certain."

"I know what you mean."

"But then I knew he wasn't so sure about things after all...and now I think I know what he was talking about when he spoke about not knowing if what we do is right or not and about hopes and fears for our children."

"Yes."

"It's time for me to come off the street, Mr Hennessey."

"Yes. I think it is," Hennessey smiled. "You are young...and tomorrow is the first day of the rest of your life...live the rest as Leonard Brogan would want you to live it."

Emily Speake returned the smile. "Yes...yes, I will, I'll do that...I'll do it for Leo."

Hennessey left the interview room and walked to the enquiry desk to pick up a statement pad. He noticed Walter Tamm sitting on the bench.

"Gentleman wishes to see you, sir." The ginger haired duty constable turned to Hennessey and indicated towards Tamm.

"Didn't expect to see you back so soon, Walter."

"Yes," Tamm shrugged. "I thought about what you said...I listened to what the solicitor said to me once we were outside. I think I'd like to work for myself on this one...I'm well out of my depth."

"Yes." Hennessey looked about him, there were no other members of the public in the area of the enquiry desk. "We're taking a statement now from somebody else which implicates you, so we would have been arresting you later today, but tell me what happened."

"The Russian girl...Luke fell for her in a big way...she didn't want any of it...Luke's used to getting what he wants, couldn't take the refusal...picked up an iron bar. She never knew what hit her."

"A young life lost for...for...*that*." Hennessey did not disguise his anger.

"Yes." Tamm hung his head. "You might not believe me, but it makes me angry as well."

Hennessey paused, leaning on the enquiry desk. Then he asked. "Was she alive when you put her in the deep freeze?"

"Yes."

Hennessey caught his breath and then grimaced.

"Unconscious...but alive. She never knew anything from the moment he hit her over the head. We moved the body because he had to sell his cottage."

"Yes, we worked that out."

Hennessey turned to the constable. "Put him in a holding room, please. For the log, his name is Walter Tamm. I am the interested officer."

"He was full of his denials and rights at first and in fact we were far from home and dry." George Hennessey and the slender woman walked arm in arm along the cliff top at Whitby in order to observe the sunset over the North Sea as folk used to do before television became the primary source of visual stimulation. An observer would note them to be middle-aged, probably still immeasurably happy in a long and successful marriage. "We still had nothing to link him to the murder itself. Walter Tamm's statement about what happened still wasn't enough in the face of Brogan's endless denials...then SOCOs came up trumps, found a human hair in the deep freeze in Ewe Cottage."

"Belonged to the Russian girl?" The woman spoke softly.

"Yes...the lab at Wetherby got a DNA match...or a 'hit' as they refer to it."

"So, in the face of that and the statements from Tamm and Emily Speake, and following advice from the duty solicitor, he went G as my son would say. By doing that he'll broker some time for himself, eat a little less porridge. Amazing sunset..."

The man and the woman stopped walking and turned to look out across a flat, calm, North Sea, underneath a sky of various hues of scarlet and crimson, which stretched like the underside of a huge blanket to the horizon.

"Red sky at night..." Hennessey said.

Turning away from the vista of the sea and the sky and looking across the harbour at the ruined abbey next to the church, Hennessey said, "Can't help feeling sorry for Walter Tamm. Didn't realise quite how out of his depth he was. Colour just dropped from his face when we told him he too would be charged with murder. He'd been cautioned of course, both on and off the record...but he confessed anyway."

"Because it wasn't the blow to the head which killed her...it was being placed in the deep freeze."

"Exactly, and in which he played an equal part."

"Well...it'll be a glorious day tomorrow, pity we have to return, but the children will be returning from the weekend with their father, as you know."

"Yes...but two days has been good."

"It's been excellent." Louise D'Acre squeezed his arm. "It's been excellent. We don't do this often enough. Shall we go back to the hotel...have an early night?"

"If you like..." Hennessey turned to her and smiled.

"I like, we can look at sunsets often enough when we are both very old and both very grey."